Also by
LISI HARRISON

Monster High

Alphas
Movers and Fakers
Belle of the Brawl
Top of the Feud Chain

The Clique
Best Friends for Never
Revenge of the Wannabes
Invasion of the Boy Snatchers
The Pretty Committee Strikes Back
Dial L for Loser
It's Not Easy Being Mean
Sealed with a Diss
Bratfest at Tiffany's
The Clique Summer Collection
P.S. I Loathe You
Boys R Us
Charmed and Dangerous: The Rise of the Pretty Committee
The Cliquetionary
These Boots Are Made for Stalking
My Little Phony
A Tale of Two Pretties

THE GHOUL NEXT DOOR

A novel by

Lisi Harrison

poppy

LITTLE, BROWN AND COMPANY
New York Boston

Poppy

Hachette Book Group
237 Park Avenue, New York, NY 10017
For more of your favorite series, visit our website at www.pickapoppy.com

Poppy is an imprint of Little, Brown and Company.
The Poppy name and logo are trademarks of Hachette Book Group, Inc.

First Edition: April 2011

Library of Congress Cataloging-in-Publication Data

Harrison, Lisi.
  The ghoul next door : a novel / by Lisi Harrison.—1st ed.
    p. cm.—(Monster High)
  "Poppy."
  ISBN 978-0-316-09911-0
  I. Title.
  PZ7.H2527Gh 2011
  [Fic]—dc22

                                            2010038306

        10 9 8 7 6 5 4 3 2 1

                RRD-C

Printed in the United States of America

For Mer Mer and our NTF

TABLE OF CONTENTS

CHAPTER ONE
PHARAOH KNOWS BEST

The amber-infused air snapped with anxiety. It crackled with anticipation. It popped with impatience. Still, Cleo refused to rest until the de Nile Palace was fit for a king, even if the staff thought she was a royal pain in the—

"Better?" asked Hasina, lifting the left corner of the papyrus banner she and her husband, Beb, had been summoned to hang.

Cleo cocked her head and took three steps back to get a fresh perspective. Outside, the rain pounded, muting the hollow taps of her strappy platforms against the limestone floor. It was perfect weather for renting movies, snuggling with Boyfriend, and—

STOP! Cleo shook the cozy image from her mind. Deuce was

no longer welcome in her thoughts *or* her screening room. Not since he took Melody Carver to the school dance last night. Besides, she had to stay focused. There would be plenty of time to plot revenge later.

Joining the tips of her thumbs, Cleo stretched out her arms like a film director lining up a shot. "Ummm…" Her latte-colored hands formed a frame through which she could scrutinize the banner's latest position. It was crucial that she see exactly what her audience would see. Because her audience expected perfection, and he was due home in—Cleo glanced at the carved sundial in the center of the great hall. *Ugh!* It was completely useless at night.

"Time check!" she called.

Beb pulled an iPhone from his white linen tunic. "Seven minutes."

High Dam!

It would have been much faster to type her message in seventy-two-point font and print it from her laser printer. But her father had no tolerance for technology. When it came to notes, lists, or birthday cards, it was hieroglyphs or the highway.

Ramses de Nile—or Ram, as Westerners called him—insisted that all under his roof honor their Egyptian heritage by writing with the ancient characters—characters that averaged twenty minutes apiece to perfect. Which is why the sign said WELCOME HOME instead of WELCOME HOME, DAD. *For the love of Geb! Who had that kind of time?*

Fortunately, the mundane task hadn't hindered her usual Saturday afternoon plans with Clawdeen, Lala, and Blue, since the three S's—sunning, spa-ing, and shopping—were no longer options. Tanning in the solarium was out because of the storm.

And the other two S's had been canceled until it became safe for them to go out in public again.

Thanks, Frankie Stein!

Since the previous night's dance at Merston High (the one that Deuce took Melody Carver to!), Salem police had been searching for a "green monster" (*Frankie!*) whose head fell off during a massive make-out sesh with Brett Redding. The RAD (Regular Attribute Dodgers) community agreed it was best for *all* of their kids to stay home, just in case.

Thankfully, her father, a renowned antiques dealer, had been on an archaeological dig and had missed the drama. He was over-protective in the best of times. What if he knew that Cleo had gone along with Frankie's plan? That she had attended the school's monster-themed costume ball dressed as a mummy—or, rather, that she had gone dressed as herself? That Blue had let her sea monster scales shine? That Lala had flashed her fangs? That Clawdeen had exposed her werewolf fur? That their goal had been to show the normies that the RADs' "eccentricities" weren't something to fear but instead something to celebrate? Cleo shuddered at the thought. If Ram knew *half* of that, he'd lock her away in some underground tomb and preserve her until the year 2200.

"'S good?" Beb managed to ask through clenched teeth that looked especially ivory against his olive-colored skin.

Was it Cleo's imagination or did the top left corner *still* seem slanted? Her chest buckled like an overwrapped corpse. She wanted to be done. She *needed* to be done. There was still wine to pour; there were appetizers to arrange and the Sharkiat play-list to cue. If she didn't free up the servants, those tasks would never be completed on time. Sure, Cleo could help, but she'd rather cut off an arm than lend a hand. After all, her father always said, "There are bosses and there are workers. Yet you, my princess, are too precious for either role." And Cleo wholeheartedly agreed. But no one said she couldn't supervise.

"Higher on the left."

"But…" Beb began. Then he quickly thought better of it. Instead, he activated the carpenter's level app on his iPhone and flipped it horizontal. He watched patiently as the digital bubble bobbed toward a verdict, his cocoa-colored lips mumbling at the screen that held his fate.

"Looks perfect to me," Hasina insisted, balancing on the gilded arm of an ancient Egyptian throne. "And Beb's measurements are usually quite accurate." She widened her dark, kohl-lined eyes for emphasis.

The woman had a point.

Sixteen years ago, Ram commissioned Beb to build a house that would have impressive "curb appeal" by Western standards and "royal palace appeal" by Egyptian standards. Months later, 32 Radcliffe Way did just that.

White and pigeon-gray, the multilevel exterior had the new-money patina of a suburban McMansion. The front door opened into a cramped wood-paneled foyer. Its walls were beige, dimly lit, and *boring*. How else could the family keep pizza delivery boys and nosy cookie-selling Girl Scouts from becoming suspicious? But on the other side of that fake foyer was a second door—the *real* door, which gave access to their true home. Where the style dial had been set to palatial.

The main hall was three stories high and capped with a lofty glass pyramid. When it wasn't raining, natural light soaked the interior like melted butter on a hot pita. When rain did fall, the rhythmic tapping lulled the inhabitants like an ambient symphony score. Colorful hieroglyphs tagged the limestone walls. Carved alabaster pots detailed the burial spots of their ancestors. And a Beb-made river, filled with water from the Nile, snaked through every room in the palace. On special occasions, Hasina would adorn the stream with glittering tea lights. Otherwise it held blue Egyptian water lilies. Tonight it had both.

"Five minutes," Beb announced.

"Hang it up!" Cleo decided with a sudden clap of her hands. Chisisi, the most timid of the family's seven cats, darted up the towering date palm that grew in the middle of the room.

"Sorry, Chi," Cleo cooed. "I didn't mean to scare you."

A quiet chime echoed through the hall. It wasn't Cleo who had scared Chisisi after all. It was—

"He's home!" Hasina shouted as she saw the crisp image of her boss in the security monitor by the real door.

"Hurry!" Cleo snapped.

Hasina pressed her corner of the banner to the column with stick-or-else urgency and then eyed her husband, prompting him to do the same. But they were too late.

"Sir!" Hasina's dark cheeks turned the color of ripe plums. She quickly stepped off the gold arm of the throne and brushed away any prints her gladiator sandals might have left behind. Without another word, she and Beb escaped to the kitchen. Seconds later, high-speed vocals exploded from the built-in speakers. With Mariah Carey's multi-octave range and Alvin and the Chipmunks' sound, Sharkiat rocked the palace with "Ya Helilah Ya Helilah."

"Daddy!" Cleo squealed, sounding both crisp and mushy, like

a melted M&M. "Welcome home! How was your trip? Do you like my banner? I made it myself." She stood proudly between the columns and waited for his response. Even though she was on the mature side of fifteen (thanks to mummification), she still craved her father's approval. And sometimes that could be harder to get than lash extensions in a desert sandstorm.

But not tonight. Tonight, Ram pushed past his assistant, Manu, and headed straight for his daughter, his arms open to *I-love-you*-this-*much* proportions.

"Sir!" Manu called, his smooth voice jagged with concern. "Your coat!"

"Princess!" Ram said, pulling Cleo into his soggy black trench and squeezing hard. Torrents of rain couldn't wash away the stale smells of an international flight and a chauffeur-driven Bentley filled with cigar smoke, or the heady musk scent of his skin. Not that Cleo minded. He could have smelled like the cats' litter box after a long drink of Nile water and she would have kept hugging him.

Gripping her shoulders, he created some distance between them and studied Cleo intensely. His lavish attention made her squirm.

Is my Herve Leger bandage dress too snug? My purple eyeliner too thick? My glitter mascara too garish? The brown henna stars on my cheekbones too small?

Cleo giggled nervously. *"What?"*

"Are you okay?" He sighed, exhaling the sweet smell of tobacco. There was something unfamiliar behind his dark, almond-shaped eyes. It was soft. Searching. Maybe even scared. In most people it would be perceived as anxiety. But in her father it looked foreign. Like some buried emotion ex⌐ archaeological dig.

Cleo smiled up at him. "Of course I'm okay. Why?"

A soft bell clanged from the dining area. The appetizers were ready. Chisisi scurried down the date palm. Bastet, Akins, Ebonee, Ufa, Usi, and Miu-Miu padded out from under the chaise and toward the hearty spread. Cleo grinned warmly at the predictability of it all. But not Ram. Worry hardened his face like a Dead Sea clay mask.

"The news is everywhere." He rubbed his temples, his salt-and-pepper hair saltier than usual. "What was that Frankie girl *thinking*? How could the Steins have let this happen? They've put our entire community in danger."

"So you *heard*?" Cleo asked. But what she really wanted to know was how *much* he had heard.

Ram pulled a rolled-up *Salem News* from his inside pocket and smacked it against his palm, putting a sharp end to their tender moment. "Did Viktor forget to add a brain to that daughter of his? Because I can't for the life of Geb figure out why—"

The appetizer bell rang again.

Suddenly, the urge to defend Frankie welled inside Cleo. Or maybe that urge was a need to defend herself? "It's not like any-one knows her name. And at school she wears all of that normie makeup, so no one recognized her. Maybe she was trying to grab the *ka* by the horns," Cleo suggested, rocking nervously in her strappy platforms. "You know, to change things."

"What kinds of *things*? She was created a month ago. What gives her the right to change anything?" he asked, lifting his gaze toward the WELCOME HOME banner. *Finally!* But his sharp features showed no signs of appreciation.

How do you know so much about Frankie? Cleo couldn't help wondering. Because, *seriously*! She had friends whose parents didn't venture farther than San Francisco. Yet they remained wonderfully oblivious to the house parties and late-night joy-rides that went on in their absence. Meanwhile, her dad goes digging for artifacts on the other side of the planet and returns more dialed in than a radio station during a ticket giveaway. It was total *ka*!

"What's with your generation?" he continued, ignoring her question. "You have no appreciation for the past. No respect for heritage or tradition. All you want to do is—"

"Sir?" Manu interrupted, his bald head glistening with rain-drops. He clutched the handle of an aluminum briefcase with such intensity that his dark knuckles had turned gray. "Where would you like this?"

While considering his answer, Ram stroked the travel-day stubble blooming on his face. After a moment, he glanced at Cleo and then gestured toward the grand double doors at the far end of the hall. Firmly gripping his daughter's elbow, he led her across the airy foyer with well-rehearsed grace, and they stepped into the throne room.

A family of falcons flapped out and headed for the date palm. The birds' pointed wings echoed throughout the palace like flags snapping in the wind.

Lit by flaming alabaster oil lamps, the hammered copper walls reflected a soft amber glow. A smooth woven reed aisle, polished by thousands of years of barefoot ancestors, led to the riser upon which their thrones sat. Cleo slid onto the purple velvet seat cushion and rested her palms on the jewel-encrusted golden armrests. Instinctively, her chin jutted forward and her eyelids lowered to half-mast. Now, with her vision slightly obscured, everything came to her in bits and pieces. She was suddenly a queen, taking dainty sips of her kingdom instead of swallowing it in one big gulp: the black-and-emerald scarab above the doorway...the bulrushes along the snaking Nile...the two ebony sarcophagi that flanked the entrance.

The sights, smells, and sounds of her kingdom banished the tension of the last couple of days and made her feel safe, especially now that its ruler had returned. Breathing became less labored, and her skin tingled with entitlement. Oh, how right royal felt.

Once they were settled, Manu gently lowered the briefcase onto the copper table between the thrones and then stepped back to await further instruction.

Open it, Ram conveyed with a mere flick of his wrist.

Manu clicked open the case, lifted the velvet-lined top, and took a long step backward.

"Behold," Ram said. "I found it in Aunt Nefertiti's tomb." He twisted his emerald thumb ring with quiet confidence.

Cleo leaned over the armrest and gasped. She immediately began taking a mental inventory of the bounty that lay glistening before her.

1. A lapis necklace fashioned in the shape of a falcon, its widespread wings meant to rest on the collarbones of Egypt's most admired women

2. Hammered cuffs joined by a ruby-and-emerald eye of Horus

3. A solid-gold vulture-shaped crown, which was so weighted down with shiny jewels that Cleo could see her wide, desire-filled eyes mirrored in every colored stone

4. A gold spiral ring with a gum ball–sized gray moonstone that practically glowed in the dark

5. Pear-shaped jade earrings wrapped in gold wire that made Angelina Jolie's 2009 Oscar emeralds look like hair baubles

6. A gold collar necklace with pearls and peacock feathers hanging off the bottom

7. A ruby-eyed snake cuff meant to wind up the arm, from wrist to bicep

8. A thick white business card jammed haphazardly beside the other contents of the case

"Wait!" Cleo leaned closer and snatched up the card. "What's this?" she asked, even though she knew. *Who wouldn't?* The ubiquitous silver logo embossed across the top of the card was a five-letter word for "major opportunity."

"*Golden,*" she whispered in awe. Quaking, Cleo read the words on the card, and the stacked bangles on her arm shook in time with the jubilant Egyptian music. "Where did you get *this?*" she asked.

Eyes still forward, Ram grinned smugly. "Spectacular, isn't it?

How do you feel about your past *now*? Do you have any idea what these are *worth*? Not just in dollars, but in history? The ring alone—"

"Dad!" Cleo jumped to her feet. The throne was no longer wide enough to contain her excitement. She rubbed her thumb over the embossed letters one at a time—V...O...G...U...E... "How did you get *her* business card?"

As Ram quickly turned to face his daughter, his raw disappointment was suddenly exposed. "What's so special about this Anna Winter?" he snapped, shutting the briefcase. Manu stepped forward to remove it, but Ram waved him away.

"Win-*tour*, Dad!" Cleo insisted. "She's the editor in chief of *Vogue*. Did you really meet her? Did you talk to her? Were her sunglasses off or on? What did she say? Tell me everything."

Ram finally wriggled out of his black trench coat. Manu hurried to retrieve it and then quickly offered him a cigar. As if delighting in his daughter's squirmy anticipation, Ram took several measured puffs before indulging her.

"She sat beside me in first class on the flight from Cairo to JFK." He released a stinky cloud of smoke from his tight lips. "She saw the article about my dig on the front page of *Business Today Egypt* and started going on and on about her newfound love of Cairo couture...whatever that is." He rolled his eyes. "She wants to dedicate a whole issue to it."

From his post behind the throne, Manu shook his head. He looked just as offended as Ram.

"She actually said 'Cairo couture'?" Cleo beamed. Egypt was finally in vogue!

"That woman said a lot of things." He clapped twice. Beb and

Hasina hurried from the kitchen balancing platters of food on the flats of their hands. Bastet, Akins, Chisisi, Ebonee, Ufa, Usi, and Miu-Miu scampered hungrily behind them.

Cleo sat. "Like what?" she pressed. "What else did she say?"

"Something about a photo shoot for her younger magazine."

Hasina lowered a bronze platter in front of him. Ram reached for a pita triangle and dipped it in a swirl of hummus.

"*What?*" Cleo gasped, waving away Beb's tray of cheese and lamb *sambouseks*. The only app she wanted was called *Teen Vogue*, and it was available on iTunes for $1.99.

"Something about models riding camels in the Oregon sand dunes wearing my sister's jewels and the latest in Cairo couture."

Cleo shifted on her throne. First she crossed her right leg over her left, then her left over her right. She shook her ankle, sat on her hands, and tapped her fingers on the plush armrest. Despite her father's intolerance for fidgeting, she couldn't help herself. Every cell, nerve, muscle, ligament, and tendon in her body was prodding her to run outside, Spider-Man up the palace walls, and shout the golden news from the rooftops. If only it were safe to leave the house.

Thanks again, Frankie Stein!

"The whole thing is exploitative, if you ask me," Manu mumbled.

Ram nodded in agreement.

Cleo shot the servant a *shut-up-now-or-I'm-going-to-cover-your-bald-head-in-goose-liver-and-call-the-cats* glare. He cleared his throat and lowered his round, liquid brown eyes.

"I want in!" Cleo insisted, batting her lashes.

"In on *what*?" Ram stubbed out his cigar in an ankh-shaped

dish of baba ghanoush. Hasina swooped in and removed it immediately. "I didn't agree to anything."

"But that didn't stop Anna Winter from organizing the entire shoot in the time it took to taxi from the runway to the gate. She even picked a date," Manu offered.

"When?"

Ram shrugged, as if he cared too little to remember. "October fourteenth."

"I'm totally free that day." Cleo jumped to her feet and speed-clapped.

Her father glanced over his shoulder and flashed Manu the same *cats-on-your-bald-head* warning. "That Anna Winter acts more entitled than a queen, for Geb's sake. I don't want to work with—"

"You don't have to do a thing. *I'll* work with her." Cleo was so excited that she didn't even try to correct their mispronunciation again. This *must* happen. It was destiny.

Ram searched his daughter's face for some sort of guidance. Despite her galloping heart, Cleo remained still and in control.

"I know!" she said with a snap of her fingers, as if she'd just thought of it. "I'll be one of the models." She looked him in the eye. "That way I can oversee the process from start to finish," she offered, knowing all too well how her father's mind worked. Ram might write in hieroglyphs and speak Egyptian, but he thought like Donald Trump. He valued initiative, confidence, and micromanagement more than anything he'd ever exhumed.

As he twirled his emerald thumb ring, his almond-shaped eyes looked distant and thoughtful.

"Please," Cleo pleaded, dropping to her knees. She bowed

until her forehead touched the carpet. It had the same musky sweetness as her Moroccan hair oil. *Pleasesayyespleasesayyespleasesayyespleasesayyes....*

"I didn't raise you to be a model," he said.

Cleo lifted her eyes. "I know *that*," she cooed. "You raised me to be a world-class jewelry designer."

He acknowledged her lifelong dream with a nod but still failed to see the point.

Cleo sat up. "What better way to network"—*impress my friends and make Deuce regret the day he ever asked Melody to the dance,* she silently added—"than to work with the accessories editor of *Teen Vogue?*"

"Why do you need to network?" Ram asked, sounding hurt. "I can get you any job you want."

Cleo wanted to stomp her platform sandals and scream. Instead, she clasped her father's hand. "Daddy," she managed to say calmly, "I descended from a queen. Not a princess!"

"What's that supposed to mean?" he asked, his eyes warming to a more playful temperature.

"It means, I want what I want." Cleo grinned. "But I can do it myself."

"Excuse me, Miss Cleo," Hasina interrupted. "Would you like me to draw your bath?"

"Lavender, please."

The handmaiden nodded and then hurried off.

Ram chuckled. "So much for wanting to do things yourself."

Cleo couldn't help smiling. "I asked her to draw the bath, not take it for me."

"Oh, I see." He smiled back. "So you want me to confirm the

shoot, insist that you get to model, and then stand back and let you do the rest?"

"Exactly." Cleo kissed her father's well-preserved forehead.

Tapping his pursed lips, Ram made one last show of considering his daughter's request. Cleo forced herself not to fidget.

"Maybe this is exactly what your generation needs," he mused.

"Huh?" This was hardly the response she had been hoping for.

"I bet if Viktor Stein had encouraged his daughter to get more involved in extracurricular activities, she wouldn't have gotten herself into so much trouble."

"I *totally* agree." Cleo nodded so hard her bangs shook. "Who has time for trouble when they're busy? I certainly don't."

Relief washed over her father's face. He lifted the business card from Cleo's fingertips and handed it to Manu. "Make the call."

Yessss! No matter how stern Ram acted, Cleo had him wrapped.

"Thanks, Daddy!" Cleo covered her father's cheek with glossy, berry-scented kisses. This was the first significant step on her path to fashion world domination. And the possibilities made her well-preserved heart soar higher than the highest WELCOME HOME banner ever hung.

Spark off, Frankie Stein. There's a new headline in town.

TO: Clawdeen, Lala, Blue

sept 26, 6:34 PM

CLEO: IGNORE CURFEW AND SNEAK OVER ASAP. SPECIAL SURPRISE. ^^^^^^^^^^^^ (BTW, LIKE MY NEW SIGN-OFF? IT'S PYRAMIDS.)

TO: Clawdeen, Lala, Blue

sept 26, 6:38 PM

CLEO: U SHOULD EACH HAVE A SPECIAL SIGN-OFF. CLAWDEEN: ##### FOR CLAW MARKS. LALA: :::::::::::: FOR FANG MARKS. BLUE: @@@@@@@ FOR SCALES. BTW, DID U GET MY LAST TEXT??? COME OVER!

TO: Clawdeen, Lala, Blue

sept 26, 6:46 PM

CLEO: I'LL HAVE MANU MEET U IN THE RAVINE IF YOU'RE SCARED. TRUST ME. IT'S WORTH IT. ^^^^^^^^^^^^

CHAPTER TWO
WAX ON, WAX OFF

Lightning snapped the night sky like a jock's gym towel on a dork's butt. The rain fell harder. Trees swayed and cracked. A pack of wolves howled in the distance. Reception on the flat-screen TV flickered and settled...flickered and settled...flickered and—

Ping!

Melody Carver curled away from her older sister, Candace, and burrowed into the corner of the eggplant-colored couch. She pressed PLAY on her phone and braced herself for another iThreat.

"Tick...tick...tick..."

It was just like the others. Recorded by her ex-friend Bekka Madden and sent to Melody's iPhone every sixty minutes, it was a haunting reminder that the forty-eight-hour deadline was now more like twenty-three.

Bekka's goal was simple: to capture the green monster who had made out with, and traumatized, her boyfriend, Brett, at the school dance. Rather, she wanted Melody to capture the monster for her. And Melody had until ten o'clock on Sunday night to do it. If she failed, Bekka would post a video of Jackson Jekyll turning into D.J. Hyde. Then he would be "wanted" too. Melody wanted to protect Jackson more than anything. But she had *met* this "monster." In fact, she had accidentally shocked Melody in the lunch line on the first day of school. And except for the whole *neck-bolts-green-skin-stitches-electricity* thing, Frankie Stein was completely normal. Strip away the heavy makeup and the nun-friendly wardrobe and she was actually quite beautiful.

Another shock of lightning lit the ravine behind the Carvers' house. Thunder boomed.

"Ahhhh!" Candace and Melody screamed.

The TV flickered and settled…flickered and settled.

"Ugh! This is so ten thousand years ago!" Candace smacked a velvety cushion. "I feel like a cave woman."

Aftershocks of frustration rippled toward Melody's corner of the couch. "I don't think they had HDTV ten thousand years ago."

"Pay attention!" Candace nudged Melody in the thigh with her pedicured foot. "I'm not talking about the TV."

"Well, what *are* you talking about?" Melody asked, focusing on her older sister for the first time all night.

Candace—wearing a dusty-rose kimono—was surrounded by strips of cloth, Popsicle sticks, anthills of baby powder, and a bowl of what looked like congealed honey. "I'm talking about this stupid leg-waxing kit! It's so primitive."

"Since when do you wax your own legs?" Melody wondered, checking her phone for any texts or tweets she might have missed during this brief exchange.

"Since last night's monster drama scared the only decent salon in town into closing on a Saturday." Candace spread a thick dollop of wax on her shin and covered it with a white rectangular strip. "If it doesn't open soon, Salem really *will* be full of scary beasts." She rubbed the strip vigorously. "I mean, have you *seen* the girls at school? I told this one chick I thought her mohair pants were super rock-and-roll, and you know what she said?"

Searchlights from a passing patrol car streaked across the log walls of the Carvers' living room as police hunted Frankie Stein with sharklike tenacity. Melody picked her jagged cuticles. How much longer would she be able to keep her cool? An hour? All night? Until Bekka's next audio threat? The clock was ticking. Time was running out.

"Mel." Candace toe-poked her again. "You know what she *said*?"

Melody shrugged, unable to take her mind off Jackson and the danger he'd be in if she didn't think of a way to stop Bekka from leaking his video—some way other than turning in Frankie. Something cunning and clever and—

"She said, 'I'm not wearing mohair pants!'" Candace reached for the wax strip on her leg. "You know why she said that? Because she was wearing a miniskirt, Melly! A miniskirt! The poor girl was *that* hairy!" She squeezed her eyes shut and ripped. "Arrrrrrgh! Hair *out*!"

Ping!

"What now?" Candace asked, drizzling baby powder over her raw skin.

Melody checked her phone. It was Jackson.

19

JACKSON: DID U SEE ARTIST SKETCH OF FRANKIE ON THE NEWS?

MELODY: NO. STORM IS MESSING UP TV.

JACKSON: LOOKS LIKE YODA IN A WEDDING DRESS.

Melody giggled.

"What is it? What's so funny?" Candace asked, swinging her long blond waves over her shoulder with the allure of a hair model.

"Nothing," Melody mumbled, avoiding her sister's searching green eyes. Was she keeping Candace in the dark to protect her? Or was she doing it to test herself? To see if she could survive this complicated situation—and maybe even triumph—without the help of her fearless, flawless sibling. She couldn't be sure.

MELODY: ANY IDEAS YET?

JACKSON: NO BUT WE NEED TO THINK OF SOMETHING. IF BEKKA SHOWS THE VIDEO, MY MOM IS GOING TO SEND ME TO LONDON TO LIVE WITH MY AUNT.

The news tore through Melody's insides with the ripping force of a wax strip. Even though they had known each other only a month, she couldn't fathom Salem without him. She couldn't fathom *anything* without him. In the English language of love, Melody was the letter Q and Jackson was her U. He completed her.

MELODY: LET'S TALK TO BEKKA! MAYBE IF WE BEG…

JACKSON: SHE'S TOO BUSY DOING INTERVIEWS. SHE'S ALL OVER TV AND WEB. SHE'S NOT STOPPING TILL SHE GETS

FRANKIE. BRETT IN SHOCK. STILL AT HOSPITAL. MAJOR VIGIL. CRAZY! VIDEOS ALL OVER YOUTUBE OF FAKE MONSTER SIGHTINGS.

Another wax strip ripped through Melody's insides. These updates were only stressing her out more. She needed to get off the couch and take action. To find a way to delete that video of Jackson from Bekka's phone and —

The front door swung open. A chilly gust of wind blasted through the cabin. It was followed by a clap of thunder.

"Ahhhh!" the girls screamed again. Candace panic-kicked her legs in the air. Her hamstrings were covered with crooked patches of white cloth.

"Who's ready for game night?" their mother called, shaking off her brown-and-gold Louis Vuitton umbrella before entering the house. "We've got UNO, Balderdash, and Apples to Apples," she announced, depositing two wet Target bags and four from Nordstrom in the kitchen sink. The only thing the ex–personal shopper detested more than blue socks with black pants was water damage on hardwood floors.

Game night? Candace mouthed silently.

Melody shrugged. It was the first she'd heard of it too.

"How about some low-fat thin-crust personal pizzas?" asked Beau, their perma-tanned, ultra-fit father. He followed Glory with a bag of takeout and a *fun-for-the-whole-family* grin.

"Dad's going to eat cheese? What's the occasion?" Candace called from the couch.

Glory appeared and handed each girl a brown shoe box

marked UGG. "We're just trying to make the best of this whole curfew thingy. We want to let loose in case this is our last night among the living." She winked playfully at Melody, making obvious her belief that this whole monster-hunt hype was just a small-town strategy for boosting sales of canned goods, bottled water, flashlights, and batteries in a slow economy. But in the spirit of fitting in, her parents had decided to play along.

Candace lifted the shoe box lid and carefully peeked inside. "Huh? You always said UGGs were the mountain man's flip-flops. And that they should never be worn by single women."

"That was when we lived in Beverly Hills," Glory explained, untying her gold silk head scarf and shaking out her auburn hair. "We're in Oregon now. The rules have changed. It's chilly here."

"Not in this house," Melody said, referring to the broken thermostat. Outside the wind was howling, yet she was sweating in boy shorts and a tank.

"Is everyone wearing their UGGs?" Beau asked, clomping toward them in a new gray pair. Despite his heavy use of Botox, the joy on his face could not be concealed.

"Why are you guys so...happy?" Candace asked, and then— *rrrrip!*—she pulled another strip off her leg. "Owie," she gasped, and then speed-rubbed the red blotch.

"We're excited for some weekend family time." Beau leaned over the back of the couch and stroked the top of his daughter's blond head. "This is the first Saturday night in years Candi hasn't had a date."

"Um, correction." Candace tightened the tie on her kimono and stood. A silver gum wrapper was stuck to the wax on her knee. "I *had* a date. It just got canceled 'cause of this stupid curfew. Now I'm stuck inside with board games, personal pizzas, and UGG boots." She pulled off the gum wrapper, crumpled it into a silver ball, and whipped it at the stone fireplace. "Forget about Candace out. From now on it's Candace *in*. Trust me, this is nothing to get excited about."

"Sor-*ry*." Glory pouted, quickly boxing up the boots. "I had no idea your father and I were so horrible to be around."

"I didn't mean it like *that*." Candace rolled her eyes.

Ping!

Melody checked her phone, grateful for an excuse to tune out the family-night family fight.

JACKSON: U STILL THERE? WHAT HAPPENED? NEED TO THINK OF A PLAN. TIME IS RUNNING OUT.

Just as Melody lifted her index finger over the touch screen, her phone was lifted from her hand.

"What are you *doing*?" she squealed at Candace.

"Trying to have a little family fun," her sister teased, taunt-waving the phone. "You've been a total text maniac all night, and I want to know what's going on."

"Melody!" Beau said sternly. "Have you been *sexting*?"

"*What?*" Melody snapped. "Ew, no!"

Under different circumstances, she might have laughed at his fatherly attempt to talk teen, but there was nothing funny about getting iJacked. "Candace, give it back!"

"Not until you tell me what's going on!" Candace insisted,

lifting the phone over her head. "Who are you talking to? Mr. Hollywood?"

"*Who?*" Melody lunged for the phone, but Candace quickly pulled it away.

"That *el mysterioso* guy who always wears a hat and sunglasses. Didn't he take you to the dance last night?"

"Not really. We were kind of forced to go together by Bekka. We didn't even hang out or—" Melody stopped herself. "Why am I even explaining this to you?"

"I knew it! It's Jackson!"

"Candace!" Melody lunged again. "Give me back my phone! Dad, get it!"

"No way," he moped. "You two are on your own." He got up and UGGed back to the kitchen, grumbling sarcastically about the joys of parenting teenage girls.

"*Can*-dace!" Melody whipped a pillow at her sister's chest, but Candace batted it aside with the finesse of someone used to fighting off foreign invasions.

"Give it now!" Melody insisted. She lunged across the couch, her fingers primed for hair pulling. Just as she was about to make contact with Candace's scalp, a puff of white powder clouded her vision.

Melody began coughing instantly.

"Stay back!" Candace warned, wielding the bottle of baby powder like a blade. "Or I'll do it again."

"My asthma!" Melody managed, waving away the baby-scented fog.

"Oh, crap, I forgot," Candace said, dropping her weapon. "Are you okay? Do you need your inhaler?"

Melody gripped her throat and nodded. The instant Candace

24

turned, Melody darted forward and ripped a wax strip off the inside of Candace's thigh. "Ha! Gotcha!"

"Ahhhh!" Candace wailed. She jumped to her feet and, with a penny stuck to the back of her calf, made a run for the sliding glass door that led out back to the ravine. "Phone out!"

"You *wouldn't*." Melody squinted.

Candace unlocked the door and made a show of sliding it open. "Tell me what's going on, or I swear this phone will be hanging like a flat-screen TV in some bird's nest."

Melody didn't dare call her bluff. The last time she tried that, her Barbie backpack had been tossed into the back of a passing convertible. Instead she gave in, just as she always did, and whispered to Candace all about Bekka, Brett, Frankie, Jackson, the video, and the ticking clock.

"Wow," Candace said after Melody had finished explaining. She handed back the phone without being prompted, cocked her head slightly, and stared. Her expression was a blend of intrigue and confusion, as if she were studying a stranger she could swear she'd met before.

Melody bit her thumbnail, terrified of her sister's reaction. *Is she going to laugh at my predicament? Call me a sucker for not turning in Frankie? Blame me for becoming friends with Bekka in the first place? Force Jackson out of my life? Tell our parents this whole monster thing* isn't *part of Salem's stimulus package after all?*

A clap of thunder broke the silence that hung between them.

"Stop staring at me," Melody urged. "Say something."

"You almost had me," Candace replied, grinning. "But the whole *Frankenstein's-daughter-hiding-out-in-her-father's-lab* thing? Seriously?" She pushed past Melody and padded back to the couch.

"Look, if you don't want to admit you and Jackson are sending love texts, that's fine. But at least come up with something more creative. You're the last person I expected to ride the monster train to Trendy Town. It's way beneath you."

Melody was about to defend herself but decided against it. Why not let Candace believe her Frankie drama was made up? That was better for everyone.

"You're right." Melody sighed and sat on the mirrored coffee table. "I was lying. I'm too embarrassed—"

"Aha!" Candace jumped to her feet. "You *were* telling the truth!"

"*What?* No, I wasn't."

"Lies!" Candace poked the thick air with an adamant finger. "You never admit I'm right when I'm actually right."

Melody giggled guiltily while marveling at the way Candace defied the dumb-blond stereotype. There was no air in that head. The spinning wheels in her brain blew it all out her ears.

"So, there really is a Frankenstein's daughter?" Candace whispered.

Melody nodded.

"And she really lives in a lab?"

Melody nodded again.

"And she's charged with electricity?"

"*Yes!*"

"Très cliché." Candace peeked at the sliding glass door that lead to the ravine. "Are there others?"

"I'm not sure," Melody said. "But you don't have to be scared." Then Melody felt compelled to explain. "They're completely normal...ish."

26

"Scared?" Candace smiled slowly, her face illuminating like a lake at sunrise. "I'm not *scared*. I'm psyched."

"Huh?" Melody brought her knees to her chest. The cold surface of the mirrored coffee table cooled her clammy feet.

"I'm proud of you." Candace grinned. "You're finally part of something dangerous."

"Really?"

"Yeah, I just can't figure out *why*," she admitted, beating white powder from the couch cushions. "It's just not like you to get involved."

Melody took offense to this comment, even if it came from the girl who thought downloading *Hope for Haiti Now* made her a humanitarian. "I guess I know what it feels like to be judged by my looks," she explained, for what felt like the hundredth time.

"And?" Candace stood, feeling the backs of her legs for leftover strips. Her tone was more curious than condescending.

Melody knew it was hard for a genetically perfect person like Candace to understand what it was like to be aesthetically challenged. Because no matter how many times she told her sister about her life pre—nose job and the abuse she got from the kids at school, it never seemed to sink in. It was like explaining Costco to a Tanzanian bushman.

"*And* I want people to stop judging," Melody continued. "Actually, I want people to stop feeling judged. Oh, and I want to stop bullies from intimidating people…or monsters…or whoever…." She stopped, knowing she sounded slightly scattered. "I just want to help, okay?"

Candace began to spin like a dog chasing its tail. "You can

start by pulling off the rest of this wax," she said. "I can't get a good grip on the ones in the back."

"Forget it," Melody mumbled. "After everything I just told you, *that's* what you're thinking about? Your *legs?*"

Ping!

Melody checked her phone. It was another audio message from Bekka. This time she listened to it on speaker.

"Tick…tick…tick…"

Bekka's freckly face popped into Melody's mind. It was a face Melody used to trust. A face she ate lunch with. The face of a friend. But now that face was smug. And it probably laughed like *mwuhhhh hahaaaa haaaaa* every time Bekka sent a stupid "tick… tick…tick" message. Melody tried to imagine her ex-friend snooping through her phone. Stumbling upon the video of Jackson. Concocting this blackmail scheme. Vilifying Frankie. Leading a monster hunt. Spreading fear and panic. Using her bruised ego as an excuse to destroy lives…

Ugh!

Melody's heart pumped harder and faster with every thought. She wanted to stand up and take action. To tear off Bekka's head the way Brett had accidentally torn off Frankie's. Melody wanted to leap off the coffee table, grab one of the wax strips on the back of Candace's precious legs, and yank out her frustration.

So she did.

"Ahhhh!" shrieked Candace.

Melody marched across the living room with a new sense of purpose. "Next time I hear that scream, it's gonna be coming from Bekka."

"Wait," Candace said, hurrying after her. "You think there are any hot ones?"

"Easy, Bella! Now who's riding the train to Trendy Town?"

"Stop!" Candace insisted. "I want to help."

This time Melody turned to face her. *Seriously?*

"Yeah." Candace nodded with genuine sincerity. "I need a cause for my college applications."

"Candace!"

"What? The more support you have from normal people, the better, right?"

Melody considered that statement for a moment. Once again, her sister had a point. Who better to fight for the rights of the aesthetically challenged than the genetically perfect? Nothing says "We're all the same on the inside" better than ACs and GPs living in harmony. Not even the movies.

"Fine. Get dressed," Melody said. "And keep it casual."

"Airplane casual or yoga casual?"

"Super casual."

"Why? Where are we going?" Candace asked, fluffing her hair.

"I'm not sure yet," Melody said, climbing the uneven wood steps to her bedroom. "But wherever it is, I'll definitely need a driver."

TO: Clawdeen, Lala, Blue
sept 26, 7:01 PM
CLEO: MORE JEWELS THAN OSCAR NIGHT. COME PLAY.
^^^^^^^^^^^^

TO: Clawdeen, Lala, Blue
sept 26, 7:06 PM
CLEO: FIRST ONE HERE GETS TO WEAR THE GOLD
VULTURE CROWN. ^^^^^^^^^^^^

TO: Clawdeen, Lala, Blue
sept 26, 7:09 PM
CLEO: YOU'LL BE SORRY. SHE WHO BAILS MUST WEAR
ZALES. ^^^^^^^^^^^^

TO: Clawdeen, Lala, Blue
sept 26, 7:12 PM
CLEO: UM, CAT GOT YOUR THUMB? WHY AREN'T YOU
TEXTING BACK? ^^^^^^^^^^^^

CHAPTER THREE
ALL CHARGED UP AND NOWHERE TO GO

Frankie Stein turned to face the caged lab rats beside her bed. "I don't have a ton of experience with this sort of thing," she said. "But isn't it customary to check up on a friend after her head falls off?"

Rat B—or Gwen, as Frankie had named her—lifted her pink nose and sniffed. Gaga, Girlicious, Green Day, and Ghostface Killah continued spooning.

"Well, if it isn't, it should be," she said, rolling onto her back. A single-bulb operating lamp hovered overhead. Like a judgmental Cyclops, it had been looking down on her for the last twenty-four hours.

Then again, who hadn't?

It had been raining all day. A sudden flash lit the street beyond the frosted-glass window. It wasn't the first bolt of lightning to strike Frankie's metal bed. But it was the strongest. The current, so pure and powerful, made her father's DIY amp-machine charge seem like a bull with a broken leg in comparison. Her legs shot up and landed with a thud. Just like her social life.

"All charged up and nowhere to go," she said with a sigh, pinching open the toothy clamps that gripped her bolts like tiny alligator jaws. Her energy had been fully restored. Her neck had been restitched. And her seams had been tightened. After losing her head during a knee-melting make-out session with normie Brett Redding, Frankie had been given a second chance at life. Unfortunately, it wasn't the life she wanted.

Breathing the formaldehyde-soaked air in her father's laboratory, Frankie missed the voltage girly touches he had stripped away after the "incident": the vanilla scented candles, the skeleton with Justin Bieber's face, the beakers filled with lip gloss and makeup brushes, the pink rugs, the red couch, the glitter on Gaga, Gwen, Girlicious, Green Day, and Ghostface Killah. All were gone. All traces of happy Frankie had been removed. In their place were sterile surgical tools, curly electrical wires, and plain white lab rats—soulless reminders of how she had come into this world. And how easy it would be to unplug and take her out.

Not that her parents *wanted* to take her out. They obviously loved Frankie. Why else would Viktor have spent all night rebuilding her? It was the rest of the Salemites who wanted to pull the plug. After all, she was to blame for the first RAD hunt since the 1930s. She had scared Brett straight to the psychiatric ward. And every police officer in town was looking for her.

But still, did her parents have to confiscate her phone? Confine her to the lab? Yank her out of Merston to home-school her? Yes, she had sneaked out of the house and gone to the dance, even though she had been (unfairly) grounded. And yes, her green skin had been (completely) exposed. And yes, yes, yes, her head (accidentally) had fallen off. But come on! She was taking a stand against discrimination. Couldn't they see that?

Thunder rumbled overhead. Gaga, Gwen, Girlicious, Green Day, and Ghostface Killah stood up on their hind legs and frantically scratched the glass walls of their cage.

Frankie reached inside. Their tiny hearts were speeding in fight-or-flight mode. But they were captives, with no options of fighting or fleeing. They were forced to stay put, no matter who threatened them. Same as Frankie.

"This will help," she said, pulling out the tiny packet of multi-colored glitter she kept tucked away under their sawdust. "Just because Dad is mad at me doesn't mean you should suffer." She pinched open the mini seal and salted the rats like fries. "*It's raining glam*," she sang, trying to seem upbeat. She sounded tone-deaf instead.

Seconds later, the animals stopped speed-clawing and settled back into their usual comma-shaped state of relaxation. But now they looked like scoops of vanilla ice cream covered in rainbow sprinkles. "Voltage." Frankie smiled approvingly. "The Glitterati are back." It was only a minor step toward restoring the lab to its usual state of fab, but it was a start.

Without a single knock or warning, Viktor and Viveka entered.

Frankie backed away from the cage and returned to her bed — the only place she still belonged.

"You're up," said her father, appearing neither pleased nor disappointed. His indifference hurt more than one hundred stitches with a dull needle.

"Good night, Frankie," her mother said wearily. She folded her arms across her black silk robe, shut her violet-colored eyes, and rested her head against the door frame.

The green pigment in her skin had faded. What once had the vibrancy of mint ice cream now looked more like pickle juice.

Frankie hurried toward them. "I'm sorry!" She wanted to give them a hug. She needed them to hug her back. But they just stood there. "Please forgive me, I promise I'll—"

"No more promises." Viktor lifted his supersize palm. His eyelids hung at half-mast. The corners of his wide mouth sagged like a sweaty gummy worm. "We'll talk in the morning."

"We need to charge," Viveka explained. "We were up all night putting you back together, and today has been..." Her voice trailed off for a moment. "Draining."

Frankie looked down at her drab smiley-face hospital gown in shame. Her parents, fully grown, rarely needed to charge. But they obviously needed a boost now, and it was her fault.

Lifting her head, she forced herself to face them. But the door was closed and they were gone.

Now what?

On the other side of the wall, Viktor and Viveka's amp machine whirred to life. Meanwhile Frankie, buzzing with more energy than Salem Electric, shuffled aimlessly across the shiny white floor longing for a life beyond her father's lab. Yearning for an update from her friends. But where were they? Had they been grounded too? Were they still her friends?

And what about Melody and Jackson-slash-D.J. Hyde? They were supposed to be working on a plan to save Frankie from Bekka. But she hadn't heard from them either...unless this was payback for putting them in harm's way. Maybe D.J. didn't even like her. Maybe Melody and Bekka were together right now, laughing. Raising glasses of bubbly normie soda and toasting their success.... *"Here's to Frankie—a bigger sucker than Lala's dad, Dracula!"*

Crawling back into bed, she wrapped the fleece-coated electromagnetic blankets around her body. "Look, Cyclops. I'm an avocado hand roll."

The lamp stared back blankly.

Loneliness blew through Frankie's insides like the first crisp breeze of fall—a chilling hint of the darkness that lay ahead.

Thunder clapped. Lightning flashed. The *tap-tap-tap-tap* of the Glitterati began again.

"It's okay," Frankie mumbled from her fleecy cone. "It's just—"

Another flash.

The streetlights snapped off. The machine on the other side of the wall stopped humming. The lab went black.

"This is total *bolt-shock*!" Frankie kicked off the blankets and sat up. "Haven't I been punished enough?"

Nervous energy crackled from her fingertips, lighting up the room. "*Vol-tage!*" she whispered with renewed appreciation for her otherwise embarrassing sparking habit.

Guided by popping yellow lights, Frankie began making her way to the door. If she could just get to her parents' bedroom before their last bits of energy drained, she could give them a jump start—a little something to carry them until the amp machine turned back on. Maybe then they'd realize how lucky they were to have her. Maybe she'd be forgiven. Maybe they'd hug her.

While Frankie was reaching for the door handle, another draft blew by. Only this one didn't feel like loneliness. It felt like wind. She turned slowly to face the chill, straining to see in the darkness. But she could see only as far as the wrinkled hem of her surgical gown and the tops of her bare green feet.

The wind blew harder.

Frankie's mouth went dry. Her bolts began to tingle. Sparks flew.

"Hullo?" Her voice shook.

The Glitterati darted back and forth across their crunchy sawdust.

"Shhh," Frankie hissed, straining to hear what she couldn't see.

Thwack!

Something slammed on the other side of the lab. A cabinet? The skeleton? The window?

The window!

Someone was breaking in!

Bekka!

Had she sent the police? Were they going to take Frankie while her parents lay helpless on their bed? Thoughts of getting hauled away with no time for good-byes made her light up like a baked Alaska....

And that's how she saw the brick speeding toward her in the dark.

Frankie assumed it could only have come from a gigantic normie mob that had formed outside. And if she remembered the story of her grandfather correctly, the normies had pitchforks, burning bales of hay, and major intolerance for electrically powered neighbors.

CHAPTER FOUR
EXTREME HOME TAKEOVER

Frankie searched for any normie mob-dodging tips her father might have implanted in her brain when he built her. But the only thing that came to her was...*duck!*

Dropping to the linoleum, she lay on her belly and starfished her arms wide to get even flatter. Steel blades of terror turned in her stomach like a ceiling fan. Her panting was animalistic. Frankie squeezed her eyes shut and—

"Looks like a half-moon tonight," whispered a male voice.

What was it about murderers and small talk?

"Just do it!" Frankie cried.

"O-*kay*," he said.

Frankie squeezed her eyes even tighter. Images of her grieving parents flashed before her. But they would probably be safer and a lot less drained once she was gone. And that thought gave her kilowatts of relief.

"Hurry! Get it over with."

The intruder placed something on the floor beside her head.

A gun? A stitch remover? A bolt extractor? She was too afraid to peek. He was standing over her. She could feel his heat. Hear him breathing. *What was he waiting for?*

"What are you *waiting for*?"

He lowered a thin sheet over the top of her drooping boy shorts. "There."

She allowed her eyes to open.

"Did you kill me?"

"*Kill* you?" He chuckled. "I just saved your butt! Literally."

Frankie sat up. "Huh?"

"You were flashing a half-moon. I covered it up." The voice suddenly sounded familiar.

"*Billy?*"

"Yeah," whispered her invisible friend.

Frankie giggled. Her fingers stopped sparking. She stood.

"I came in through the window. I hope you don't mind," he said from somewhere in the darkness.

"Not at all." She beamed. "What are you doing here?"

"I wanted to check up on you," he said sweetly. "And bring you this." He placed something in her hand. It was the speeding brick. Only it wasn't a brick. It was a box wrapped in silver paper.

"What is this?" Frankie asked, tearing off the wrapping. A white rectangle lay in her palm. "An iPhone?"

"The iPhone 4, to be exact. I've been trying to call you, but a recording said your phone was no longer activated, so I thought you could use it."

"How did you—"

"Claude picked it up for me," he stated.

38

"But it's so expensive."

"It's not like I spend my allowance on movies or anything. I get in for free. And as far as clothes…"

"Ew!" She giggled as she realized that Billy walked around naked all the time. Otherwise, everyone would see a pair of pants floating around town.

"Turn it on," he said, derailing her train of thought.

Frankie pressed the dark circle at the bottom of the device. A chartreuse orchid appeared, glowing on the screen.

"That's a picture of me, holding a green flower. You can change it if you want." He clicked through to a page of colorful icons and then the address book. "I loaded it with everyone's phone numbers and contact info." He tapped an orange square. A seemingly endless list of album titles appeared. "And music, of course."

Frankie stared at the gift, searching for something to say. It wasn't the bolt-tingling technology that left her speechless. Nor was it the library of music, the pages of apps, or the packed address book. It was the kindness. "It's so mint, Billy. Thank you."

"It was nothing," he said, even though it so wasn't. "Oh, check this out. When the power went out, I downloaded a candle app. So you can see in the dark."

Frankie touched the screen. Digital warmth flickered around her. "This is beyond voltage," she said, pressing the phone to her heart space. "What did I do to deserve it?"

"Everything. You took a chance for us. And even though it kind of backfired, we're all really grateful."

"All?" The spinning steel blades in her stomach began to slow down. "So, no one's mad at me?"

"A few of the parents are, but not us. The whole Brett freak-out thing was actually kind of funny."

Frankie smiled with her entire body. If relief were electricity, she could have lit the entire country. "Thanks so much, Billy," she said to the darkness. "I'd totally hug you but..."

"Yeah, the whole naked thing," he said. "I get it."

Frankie giggled.

"By the way, where are your parents?" he asked.

"Oh, um, they're out," Frankie said, pun intended.

"When do you expect them back?"

"Sometime tomorrow."

"Perfect," Billy said, activating the candle app on his own phone. He aimed it at the frosted window.

"What are you doing?" Frankie asked, her paranoia resurfacing. Was this a trap?

"It's okay," Billy said, still aiming. "Watch..."

All of a sudden, the window creaked open. One by one, her RAD friends began slipping inside.

"It wasn't safe to meet under the carousel, so we thought we could gather here," Billy explained. "I hope it's okay."

Once again, his kindness left her speechless. So Frankie raised her digital candle alongside his and showed him how absolutely "okay" it was.

TO: AT&T
sept 26, 7:43 PM
CLEO: DO BLACKOUTS AFFECT CELL SERVICE?

TO: AT&T
sept 26, 7:43 PM
CLEO: WHAT ABOUT TEXT MESSAGES?

TO: AT&T
sept 26, 7:43 PM
CLEO: CAN U STILL RECEIVE WHEN THE POWER IS OUT?

TO: All Contacts
sept 26, 7:44 PM
CLEO: HIGH DAM! WHERE IS EVERYONE???

FROM: Manu
sept 26, 7:44 PM
PLEASE REFRAIN FROM TEXTING. SERVER IS JAMMING.
FIREWALL IS UP. COMMUNICATION TO AND FROM THE
PALACE HAS BEEN BLOCKED FOR YOUR PROTECTION.
FATHER'S WISHES.

TO: Manu
sept 26, 7:44 PM
CLEO: SO HOW ARE WE TEXTING RIGHT NOW?

FROM: Manu
sept 26, 7:45 PM
MOMENTARY LAPSE IN FIREWALL. MANU'S WISHES. ☺

TO: Manu
sept 26, 7:46 PM
CLEO: PHEW. CAN YOU KEEP IT DOWN FOR 1 MIN? OUR SECRET.

FROM: Manu
sept 26, 7:46 PM
REFRAIN FROM TEXTING!

TO: Manu
sept 26, 7:47 PM
CLEO: ☺

CHAPTER FIVE
SEALED WITH A HISS

Cleo canceled the lavender bath, opting for something far more luxurious. Kneeling on an emerald-green cushion by the foot of her bed, she laid the vintage bling on her tightly tucked linen duvet. Its old-world glamour was even more beguiling with the twinkle of candlelight reflecting in the stones. Even the cats knew this was major. Lying head to tail, they formed a furry fortress around the jewels, each one guarding the royal treasures as if its nine lives depended on it.

At first, Cleo had cursed the blackout. She couldn't possibly model for Bastet, Akins, Chisisi, Ebonee, Ufa, Usi, and Miu-Miu in the *dark*. But Hasina had appeared with a box of one hundred amber-scented votives. And when Beb had finished lighting them, Cleo's two-story bedroom was transformed into an ancient temple. The flickering light cast dancing shadows on the stone walls. And it became easy to imagine she was Aunt Nefertiti, illuminated by Ra's flame and the glow of natural beauty. Alone on the banks of the Nile, she was awaiting a secret rendezvous with a desert-hot prince named Khufu. As usual, his discerning eye would study her beauty from every angle. She had to look her best.

Cleo lifted the collar necklace. The falcon in the center almost looked alive. Its ruby eyes glittered as if it were about to leap off onto some poor unsuspecting rabbit. Next she struggled to raise the heavily adorned crown. Fifteen bicep curls on each side and she'd have Michelle Obama arms by Monday.

"What's the point?" She sighed, placing the jewels back in the case. The Aunt Nefertiti fantasy could satisfy her glamour-amour for only so long. What she needed was a *real* admirer. A modern-day prince. But she wasn't talking to *him* right now. So she was stuck with a litter of snore-purring watchcats.

Cleo padded down the steps of her sleep loft and crossed the bridge to her sandy island. The trickling Nile water always soothed her. Kneeling, she placed her hands together in prayer and lifted her blue-topaz eyes toward the moonless sky beyond her glass ceiling. She had some urgent questions for the ancient goddess of beauty.

"O Hathor," Cleo began, "why bless me with an abundance of gorgeousness and then deprive me of people to envy it? Especially on a Saturday night?" She was about to expound on the unfairness of Salem's newly imposed curfew and how she shouldn't have to suffer for Frankie's mistake. But Ram always insisted she look for solutions, not sympathy, and Hathor was probably no different.

"Okay, so here's my real question," Cleo continued. "Does Ra, god of the sun and fire, control fire*walls* too? Because I really need him to remove my dad's firewall so I can send out a few texts. Two minutes, max. And then he can put it right back up. Manu did it in, like, five minutes. So Ra could probably do it in half that time. I mean, seriously..." She lifted the steel case of jewels so that Hathor could get a better view. "What's the point of having all this beauty if no one's around to admire it?"

Hathor didn't respond.

Cleo lowered the case. "Exactly. There isn't one."

"*I'll* admire it," said a familiar voice.

Bastet, Akins, Chisisi, Ebonee, Ufa, Usi, and Miu-Miu lifted their heads.

Omigeb!

Cleo smiled at the sight of Boyfriend leaning casually against the gilded doorway of her bedroom. Yet she refused to cross the bridge and greet him.

Dressed in dark-wash skinny jeans, a deliciously faded navy long-sleeve tee, and the chocolate-brown leather high-tops Cleo had bought him for Labor Day, he put the Deuce in seduce.

Thank you, Hathor!

A descendant of the Gorgons, Deuce had snakes for hair and the ability to transform whatever he looked at into stone—hence, the hat and sunglasses. Although the accessories were crucial to the welfare of others, Cleo nevertheless appreciated the flair they added to his otherwise unassuming style. Granted, the dark lenses made gazing into Deuce's eyes impossible, but their reflection enabled Cleo to gaze into her own eyes. And that never got old.

"Cool ambience."

Cleo ran her fingers lazily through the sand to avoid looking eager. "What are you doing here?" she asked with royal attitude, just in case he'd forgotten she was mad at him.

"I tried calling," he said, stuffing his hands in his front pockets. "But you kept sending me to voice mail."

Kept?

Cleo wanted to know how *many* times he had tried. What time of day, what he would have said had he gotten through, whether her absence made his heart grow fonder. But she didn't dare tear down the facade. Why tell him that Ram had cut her service? Instead, she decided to let Deuce think she had ignored him on purpose. It gave her major aloof-appeal.

"So...what?" Deuce mumbled. "You're not talking to me?"

Unable to breathe in her gut-gripping Herve Leger for one more second, Cleo stood. The purple bandage dress minimized her mini waist and maximized her cleavage—proving the French designer to be quite a Geb in his own right.

"What exactly would you like to talk about?" she asked, placing a hand on her hip and jutting out her shoulder. Why not let him see what taking that fashion-backward girl to the dance was costing him?

"I want you to know that I have zero feelings for Melody."

"Who?" Cleo asked, checking her wonderfully moisturized cuticles. "Oh, you mean that *thing* whose only formfitting piece of clothing is a hair elastic."

Deuce shook his head and was probably rolling his eyes behind his sunglasses. He hated cattiness. But, hey, if he was going to act like a dog...*me-owwww!*

Finally, he stepped toward Cleo. Flickers from one hundred amber-scented candles licked his deeply tanned skin. "I wanted to go with *you*, remember? I asked *you* to go with me. But *you*

46

decided to boycott because of the"—he paused to make air quotes—"offensive theme."

"So you went with *her*?"

"I was forced into it by her pushy friend Bekka. I didn't *want* to. And it was the worst night ever."

Cleo longed to hear how unbearable his night was without her. When it came to Deuce, she was a love camel—storing reassurance in her invisible heart-shaped hump, dipping in when her insecurities needed to be fed, rationing his words to get her through the dry patches. "You look cute" could feed her until noon. "I'll miss you" might last a weekend. "I love you" was good for three days. But his betrayal had drained her supply. She needed a major refill.

"So, why was it 'the worst night ever'?" she asked, attempting to sound bored by the topic. The less she appeared to need, the more she got.

Deuce looked down at his Varvatos shoes. "Melody could tell I wasn't that into her. So she tried flirting and..."

"And what?" Cleo demanded with a slight tilt of her neck. The subtle movement brought a tiny undulation to her lacquer-glossy black hair.

"She took off my glasses."

Cleo gasped, recalling the oddly placed witch statue propped up against a table in the gym. "*You* did that?"

Deuce nodded shamefully. "I bolted as fast as I could, and that's when I saw you and...anyway, you know the rest. Nothing happened. I swear on Adonis."

"I dunno." Cleo sighed. His answer was so unsatisfying. He was supposed to say it was the worst night ever because he wasn't with *her*, not because he stoned some witch. It didn't matter that Cleo believed that nothing had happened between him and Melody. She wanted more reassurance anyway. Kind of like the time she bought the same pair of wedges in four different colors. If she could *have* more, why not *take* more? "Maybe we should start seeing other people."

"Huh?" he said, jamming his hands in his front pockets. "But I don't want to be with anyone but you."

Bon appétit!

Cleo could have stopped there. She'd be feasting on that admission until Monday. Instead, she sighed, milking him like a Starbucks barista.

"So, are we good?" Deuce asked, ambling toward the bridge with a tentative swagger.

Cleo looked down and brushed the fine white sand off her dress. Barefoot, she slowly made her way across the cool stone archway. Once she reached the other side, she leaned back against the railing and folded her arms across her chest. The cats settled around her ankles.

"How about now?" Deuce asked, stepping toward her and clutching a thin red box. MONTBLANC was written on the top in gold letters, and it had been poked full of tiny holes. It might as well have said GARAGE SALE.

Now face-to-face with Deuce—and her own reflection—Cleo fixed the gap in her bangs and then accepted his gift. But not his apology. Not yet.

"Open it." He grinned. "Slowly."

Cleo lifted the hinged box top. It creaked in protest. She gasped at what lay inside.

"Cool, right?" Deuce said, sliding his index finger under a delicate iridescent snake and lifting it toward Cleo's arm. The snake's silver scales caught the candlelight and reflected a kaleidoscope of rainbow-colored shifting sparkles that rivaled Aunt Nefertiti's jewels. "She came from my mom. It was her first gray hair."

Cleo leaned closer. "Hi there," she cooed into the box. "What's your name?"

The snake responded by lifting her triangular head and flicking her forked tongue. "Hsssssssssssssssssssssssssssstttttttttttt."

"*Reeeee-owww!*" meowed Bastet, Akins, Chisisi, Ebonee, Ufa, Usi, and Miu-Miu. The cats scattered like beads on a broken menit necklace.

"Hissette," Cleo gushed like a proud mother. "I'm going to name you Hissette."

Hissette flicked her tongue approvingly.

"Where do you want her?" Deuce asked, stroking the top of the snake's tiny triangular head with the tip of his thumb.

Cleo pointed to her right bicep. After her daylong hieroglyph-writing marathon, it was slightly more toned than the left.

Deuce coiled the snake three and a half times, maintaining the configuration as he slipped Hissette onto Cleo's arm. The snake's pearly silverness popped against Cleo's dark skin like a swirl of cream in black coffee.

"Deucey, she's absolutely *royal!*"

"Glad you like her. Now close your eyes."

"Closed."

The flames of one hundred amber-scented candles continued to twinkle in the darkness behind her lids. Was it an optical illusion? Or love reignited?

"Okay," Deuce said. "All done."

Cleo blinked her false-lashed lids open.

"Here's your rock," Deuce said, proudly tapping the now-solid Hissette on Cleo's arm.

"Is she dead?" Cleo asked, petting the snake's pebble head.

"No, just stoned," he said, grinning. "She'll wake up in a few hours feeling refreshed."

Cleo beamed.

"Forgive me now?" He smiled.

"On one condition," she pressed.

Deuce nodded expectantly.

"From this moment on, we are completely exclusive. No more breaks during your family trips to Greece. No more substitute dance dates. And no more Melody."

He placed one hand on his heart and lifted the other in a show of promise.

Golden!

Cleo's lashes fluttered forgiveness. Her modern-day prince had arrived.

She leaned toward him, lips pursed.

Deuce opened his mouth.

Cleo leaned closer...

"We'd better go."

She opened her eyes. "*Go?* Where?"

"Haven't you been reading your texts?"

"Um, yeah," Cleo lied, still unwilling to fess up about the firewall.

"Then we should go."

"I can't just *go*! You haven't even seen my new jewels yet," she insisted, grinding her feet into the reed mats. "Besides, what about the curfew? My dad won't let me leave. Especially with you.... Wait, how did you get up here, anyway? He'd never let—"

Deuce pressed the bridge of his Ray-Bans. "My glasses kind of slid off when Manu answered the door." He smirked.

"He's *stoned?*" Cleo gasped.

"They all are. It was the only way I could get you out of here."

"Deuce!" Cleo stomped her foot, unsure of whether to be angry or amused.

"They'll be fine in a few hours, don't worry." Deuce nudged her toward the door. "Come on. We have to get moving."

For once, Cleo allowed herself to be led. Usually she would have put up a bigger fight and insisted on knowing where they were going. But why spoil the surprise? He was dishing out romance at an all-you-can-eat buffet. And Cleo was famished.

TO: Melody, Jackson
sept 26, 7:51 PM
FRANKIE: IT'S FRANKIE. COME OVER ASAP. TAKE THE RAVINE. IT'S SAFE. MY WINDOW IS OPEN. XXXX

TO: Frankie
sept 26, 7:51 PM
MELODY: NEW PHONE? DO U HAVE A PLAN? WHERE R UR PARENTS? U OK?

TO: Melody
sept 26, 7:51 PM
FRANKIE: HURRY! XXXX

TO: Jackson
sept 26, 7:51 PM
MELODY: WHAT'S GOING ON?

TO: Melody
sept 26, 7:52 PM
JACKSON: NO CLUE. MEET IN RAVINE BEHIND UR HOUSE IN 2 MINUTES?

TO: Jackson
sept 26, 7:52 PM
MELODY: PARENTS R IN LVNGRM. THEY'LL SEE ME THRU WINDOW. I'LL COME 2 U.

TO: Melody
sept 26, 7:52 PM
JACKSON: NOT SAFE 4 U 2 X THE STREET. COPS
EVERYWHERE.

TO: Jackson
sept 26, 7:52 PM
MELODY: BETTER THEY FIND ME THAN U. ON MY WAY.

CHAPTER SIX
THE LONE NUDI

The blackout had been a miracle.

Six fuel-burning lanterns had been placed strategically through-out the Carvers' cabin. White flames offered a taste of brightness to a home starving for light.

Creeping from one dim patch to the next, Melody made it undetected to her post by the front door. Now, hidden in a pool of blackness, she gripped the brass knob and waited for her sister's signal.

The decision to clue Candace in to her whole *Bekka-leaking-Jackson's-video-to-the-press* stress was turning out to be very beneficial to the cause, which Candace insisted on naming NUDI, or Normies Uncool with Discriminating Idiots.

"What about something more respectable, like WAR—We're Against Racism," Melody tried.

Candace rolled her eyes. "Might as well call it BORE—Boring Oregon Racist Eliminators. I mean, seriously, Melly, perception is everything," she explained with authority she didn't have.

"WAR isn't a term people want to be associated with. But NUDI? Who wouldn't want to be part of *that*?"

"Um, *me*." Melody giggled. And then she noticed Frankie's urgent text. The debate was over. It was time for their first mission—a mission Candace had code-named NUDI Escape. And it was set to launch in three…two…one….

"Mommmm?" Candace shouted from the top of the stairs. "Daaaaaaad?"

Shielded by her sister's piercing voice, Melody turned the squeaky knob. The front door clicked open. A storm's sound track blared outside.

"Yes?" they answered together.

"Melly went to sleep and I'm bored! You wanna play UNOOOOOOOOOOOOO?"

"Sure!" Glory called from the living room, sounding suspicious but pleased.

"I said, 'You wanna play UNOOOOOOOOOOOOOOOOO?'"

"Yes!" her mom called again.

"UNOOOOOOOOOOOOOOOOOOOO!"

Giggling as she closed the door behind her, Melody no longer questioned her sister's dedication. For Candace, UNO with the parents on a Saturday night was the ultimate sacrifice—proof positive that she was more than a player. She was a *team* player.

Outside, the street was chilly and silent. Murky blackness fringed with rain covered Radcliffe Way like a soggy wool poncho. The porch swing creaked in the wind. Branches blew and wet leaves slapped together. Candles flickered behind the neighbors' dark windows. Just like the night before, when cans had rattled around her feet in the abandoned school parking lot, Melody felt as though she'd stepped onto the set of some tragically uninspired cliché horror film. Still, she wasn't afraid—at least, not for herself.

Pausing on the porch, she listened for the wet *whoosh* of a police car driving by.

Nothing.

It was time.

The wind picked up to a squall. With a flip of the hood of her black sweatshirt, she jumped down the cabin steps, sloshed over the wet lawn, and bolted across the road, quickly soaking her pink Converse.

Once behind Jackson's cheery white cottage (which projected optimism even at the bleakest of times), Melody dipped into the ravine.

"What took you so long?" he whispered from somewhere deep inside the bushes.

"Where are you?"

"Follow the glow-in-the-dark heart," he said, not even stopping for a kiss hello.

"*Wha—?*" Melody began. "Oh," she smiled, spotting the neon green sticker of the human heart on the back of his baseball cap.

"It came in a box of cereal," he said, stepping over a patchwork of fallen twigs and glistening leaves. "It's less conspicuous than a flashlight."

"True," Melody panted, trying to keep up. "How did you sneak out?"

"I didn't. My mom knows I'm gone."

"She *let* you?"

"We have a new truth pact," Jackson whispered. "No more secrets. Total trust. I told her Frankie needed my help, and she said okay. She's big on the whole community support thing."

Suddenly Melody wondered why she hadn't thought of that. Her parents had always been open and honest with her. Maybe she'd tell them in the morning...if the cops didn't bust her first.

"Wasn't she worried?" Melody asked.

Finally, Jackson turned to face her. His geek-chic glasses were spotted with rain. "Freaking was more like it. But I said the only way I could forgive her for not telling me about"—he cut himself off in case anyone was listening—"*you-know-what* was if we had full disclosure from here on out."

And Melody did know what. She knew it all. That he was a RAD. That he was a descendant of Dr. Jekyll and Mr. Hyde. That a chemical in his sweat made Jackson transition into D.J. Hyde. That D.J. was impulsive. That he was a music-loving life-of-the-party kind of guy. And that *that* was not the life for Melody. So she had to do everything she could to keep Jackson from overheating.

"Maybe we should rest for a while," she suggested.

He ignored her suggestion and continued walking. "My mom told me there are other RADs at our school. It's not just me and Frankie, you know. How cool is that?"

A gust of wind shook the drops off the leaves overhead. Cool rainwater spattered Melody's cheeks. More than the surprise shower, or even the news about the existence of other RADs, it was the sudden pinch of jealousy that caught her off guard. What if he wanted to hang with RAD girls instead of her? They were probably more interesting, and they definitely had more in common with him.

"Will you please slow down!" she snapped, smacking a branch with the indignation of someone who had just been dumped. "What's the rush?"

"The *rush*?" Jackson snapped back. "Frankie's house is at the end of the ravine, and the cops are everywhere. They'll arrest anyone out past curfew and take him to the station for questioning. A little nervous sweat and the heat of an interrogation light and '*Hello*, you-know-who'!"

Melody raised her eyebrows and folded her arms across her chest. She had never seen him lose his temper before.

"Sorry," Jackson said, the crackle behind his hazel eyes calming to a sizzle. "My mom has been stressing. Maybe it's rubbing off on me." He stepped closer. "Besides, if I get caught, who's gonna do this?" He leaned forward and gave Melody a long, soft kiss. Sincerity coated her lips like salve.

Take that, RAD girls!

With renewed hope, Melody offered her hand. "We'd better hurry."

He pulled her through the thicket, the neon-green sticker on the back of his hat marking her path. Scrambling to keep up no longer felt like chasing—more like following her heart.

"D, why are you going so fast?" a girl whisper-shouted in the distance.

Jackson and Melody froze like frightened bunnies.

"Ahhhh, I just got treed on!" she whined. "My hair is soaked."

"Shhh," said a boy. "It's just hair."

"Spoken by the guy in a *hat*."

Jackson put his lips against Melody's ear. "Is that Deu—"

She covered his mouth, goose bumps dotting her arms like Braille.

"*Quiet!*" insisted the boy. "Are you trying to get us killed?"

"No, *you* are," the girl hissed.

"C'mon, we're almost there."

Their tromping footsteps got louder...closer...

Bzzzzzzzzzz.

Jackson's eyes widened in horror.

"Sorry," Melody mouthed, quickly reaching into the back pocket of her AG jeans and shutting down her vibrating cell. She didn't need to check the screen to know who'd sent the message. Her heart, now used to Bekka's hourly audio texts, beat in time with the message.

Tick...tick...tick...

Thu-thump...thu-thump...thu-thump...

Tick...tick...tick...

Thu-thump...thu-thump...thu-thump. The footsteps were getting closer....

Melody peeked at Jackson slowly, wondering if the sound of her shifting eyeballs would give them away.

His jaw clenched in tiny pulses.

She gripped his hand, assuring him that everything would be okay. As if she knew.

Finally, after several petrifying seconds, the other couple was gone.

Melody and Jackson ran the rest of the way in adrenaline-fueled silence.

Ghostly images drifted back and forth behind the frosted-glass window of Frankie's bedroom. The familiar smell of amber perfume hovered around the rectangular opening like a warning. Melody couldn't place it, but something about it made her feel uneasy.

"Are you sure this is safe?" she asked, wishing her parents knew where she was.

"No." Jackson sighed, surveying the dark cul-de-sac. "Maybe I should go first."

Melody didn't argue.

Stepping on a conveniently placed tree stump, he lifted himself up to the window the way someone might get out of a swimming pool, and then wiggled inside. His suede desert boots landed with a flat *thwack*.

The rain picked up again.

"Come on," Jackson said, offering his hand. "Quick."

Melody shimmied her body through the narrow opening. Jackson gripped her ankles and eased her through like a doctor delivering a baby. Her sopping Converse landed with the same flat *thwack*.

The lab that she had visited the night before with D.J. was now teeming with kids from Merston High. Despite the dim candle-light, she was able to recognize most of them but didn't know any by name. Some wore pajamas; others wore sweats. Some stood in tight conversation clusters; others sat on the floor like delayed passengers at an airport. Some talked freely; others bit their fingernails. But they all soon had one thing in common:

The instant they noticed Melody, they stopped what they were doing and looked to one another for an explanation.

"What's going on?" Melody asked Jackson.

He took off his baseball cap and mussed his brown hat hair back to life. "Not a clue."

"Voltage! You're here," Frankie said with the gracious smile of a birthday girl. Melody was thankful for the hostess's approval. At the very least, everyone would know she had been invited.

Conversations halted. Faces turned.

Melody's heart rate accelerated. "I thought you wanted us to come over because you came up with a plan," she said, thrown by the unexpected gathering. "Because time is running out. Bekka will be—

"It's okay. I figured it all out," Frankie assured her. "I've been waiting for you to get here so I could share."

"Then what are *they* doing here?" Jackson asked, eyeing the others. "Wait! They don't know about my video, do they? I thought we were going to keep this just between us."

"They *are* us." Frankie winked.

"What?" Jackson asked, confused.

"They're RADs."

"RADs?" he mouthed silently, resting his hand on Frankie's green shoulder, which was bare thanks to a chicly belted, drooping hospital gown. "No waaaaaaay!"

As Melody scanned the candlelit crowd, her skin prickled with a mix of fear and exhilaration. She saw the pale girl from her English class...the pretty girl with the auburn curls and fur boa...the bubbly blond Australian with the glove obsession... the cute J.Crew jocks Candace had flirted with the day they arrived in Salem...omigod, DEUCE! *Did I really make out with two monsters in one month?*

"*Everyone?*" Melody asked.

Frankie nodded with delight.

"This is amazing!"

"Yup," Frankie said proudly, hugging Jackson tighter than Spanx. "Can you believe it?" she asked him.

Jackson shook his head from side to side, too overwhelmed to speak.

The girl with the boa stared at Melody while whispering to the girl with the gloves. Deuce said something to the J.Crew brothers that prompted them to step closer to Melody. Someone tapped Melody on the shoulder. She turned around, but no one was there. Cleo and her friends giggled from a distance.

Melody reached for Jackson's hand, but he didn't seem to notice. It hung clammy and lifeless in her grip, no longer responsive to her touch. He was in Frankie's arms now. Probably evaluating his future friends. Uninspired by Melody's predictable gene pool. In search of something more diverse...

Omigod! What if their entire relationship was a sham, designed to let him keep tabs on the meddling new girl? Maybe she had been lured there as a normie hostage—her life in exchange for the Jackson video?

It was a trap!

Panic stirred her blood to rapids. Fear set off alarm bells in her ears. Adrenaline pushed Melody out of the driver's seat and grabbed the wheel. With shaky force and little thought, she pulled Frankie away from Jackson, held her by the wrists, and glared into her eyes. "I know what you're trying to do, and it's not going to work!"

Heads turned again.

Frankie pouted, giggling. "You can't blame me for trying. D.J. already knows everyone here and—"

"*D.J.?*"

"Is that what all the hugging was about?" Jackson asked, pulling away and turning on his mini fan. "You were trying to make me sweat?"

Frankie nodded guiltily. "I want D.J. to hear my announcement."

Adrenaline gave the wheel back to Melody and slipped out, embarrassed. "So I'm not a hostage?"

Jackson looked at her with bemusement. Frankie burst out laughing. Her mint-green skin was extra smooth now that her stitches had been tightened.

"You're healing so quickly," Melody said in an awkward attempt to start over. "My dad's patients take weeks to recover."

"Really? What does he do?" Frankie asked with genuine interest.

"Plastic surgeon," Melody grumbled, pointing at her new and much-improved nose.

"No way!" Frankie put her arm around Melody's shoulder and pulled her close. "We have so much in common!"

Really?

Cupping her chin in her hands, Frankie batted her lashes. "Face by Dad-deee!" She beamed. Her ability to accept the strangeness of it all with such humor and grace put Melody at ease.

"*Oof!*" Someone smacked Jackson on the back, pitching him forward. "It's good to finally have you in the mix, ya two-faced freak."

Melody strained but couldn't see anyone in the dark. "Who said that?"

Jackson fumbled to straighten his lopsided glasses.

"Meet Billy." Frankie gestured to the vacant space beside her. "He's invisible. And the most voltage friend a girl could have." She kissed the air. "Just don't hug him, 'cause he's nakie," she added, giggling.

"Welcome," Billy said. A roll of Starburst appeared from thin air. A cherry candy was revealed briefly before it disappeared into Billy's mouth.

"Thanks." Jackson smiled at the hovering wrapper.

"C'mon, I'll introduce you to everyone," Billy said, tugging Jackson into the center of the lab. Jackson looked back at Melody with an expression of dread, yet he made no effort to stay. So she let him go.

"This is so cool," Melody said to Frankie, trying to show the gawkers that she could hold her own without Jackson, even though she was completely faking it. Maybe if she introduced herself, showed that her interest was genuine, asked all of them who they were, what they did, who they descended from, and why they—

"What in Geb's name is *she* doing here?" Cleo asked with amber-scented vitriol.

No wonder that smell had made her uneasy! From the moment they first met, Cleo had treated Melody like a middle-school loser; it was a soul-searing feeling that was all too familiar.

"Wait!" Cleo stomped her platform sandal. "Don't tell me *she*'s a—" Frankie shook her head.

"So, why is she here?"

Deuce ambled over with a lit candle. "No way!" He chuckled coolly. "You're a RAD?"

Cleo elbowed him. "No."

"So, why is she here?" he mumbled. Cleo glared at Frankie for the answer.

"Because I have an announcement to make, and I want Melody to hear it."

"Any other moles in the room I should know about?" Cleo asked, twirling an iridescent snake bangle on her upper arm.

"*Cleo!*" Frankie pleaded. "She's my friend."

Melody's insides warmed.

"*Stein*," Cleo huffed, "we can't trust *her*! You're putting us in even more danger."

Frankie sparked. "Actually, I'm about to do the opposite." She winked at Melody and then walked over to the operating table.

Cleo yanked Deuce toward the front of the crowd, leaving Melody alone by the window.

"Can I have your attention, please?" Frankie whisper-called. She pressed her hands on the steel slab and lifted her tiny frame up to sit. Her bare feet swung like a child's, but the somber expression behind her eyes was serious and adult.

"First," she said, "I want to thank Billy for bringing everyone." They began to applaud. Frankie waved her hands, urging them to stop. "Shhh," she reminded them, with a finger to her lips.

Wind whistled through the crack in the window, chilling the back of Melody's neck. Jackson waved for her to join him in the tightly packed group, but she shook her head. The chill was a comforting reminder that an escape hatch was only inches away.

"And thank you all for coming," Frankie continued. "I know

how dangerous it is to go out right now, so it means megawatts that you're here. I seriously thought you all hated me." She giggled.

Melody grinned, tickled by her new friend's disarming honesty.

Frankie sighed. "Last night," she said, growing serious, "I kinda..."

"Lost your head?" joked one of the J.Crew jocks. His brothers high-fived him.

Frankie reached for her neck stitches but must have thought better of it and lowered her hand. "I feel terrible that your lives are in danger because of something I did. I'm so sorry. I want things to change around here. I want to stop sneaking around ravines during blackouts. I want to stop wearing normie-colored makeup to school. I want us to be proud of who we are and to be accepted by—"

"*Melodork?*" Cleo shouted, pointing at Melody, whose cheeks burned.

The RADs snickered, quietly at first, but their laughter quickly escalated into hysterics. Not so much because they thought Cleo was funny but because she had said what they were thinking, and they clearly needed the release.

Suddenly, Jackson appeared by Melody's side and hooked his finger through her belt loop for support. She was too terror-stricken to thank him.

"Hey, aren't you besties with Bekka?" called a girl with a frosty expression.

"Check her phone!" shouted a beak-faced boy. "I bet she's tweeting about us right now."

"She's a spy!"

Melody's mouth went dry. "No! Bekka and I aren't friends anymore," she managed, her voice raspy and unsteady. "I'm new here. When I met her, I had no idea what she was like. Believe me, I want to take her down just as much as you do."

"Yeah, right," said a boy with big feet and shaggy black hair. "She's probably on her way over here right now with a TMZ crew thanks to *you*."

Melody gulped. Suddenly, breathing felt like sipping pudding through a straw.

Cleo grinned like a Cheshire cat. All she had to do was plant the seed, stand back, and watch their hate grow.

It's not like that, Melody wanted to shout back. *Bekka turned on me too! I'm more like you than you know. Don't look at my symmetrical face. Look in my eyes! I know what it feels like to be judged!* But her voice—the one that used to sing in recitals and star in musicals before she got asthma—was gone. It was curled up in a fetal position at the bottom of her throat, afraid to come out. Afraid of getting teased and bullied all over again. Afraid of ruining her last chance to start over.

"Melody is on *our* side," Jackson declared.

"Get her out of here!" shouted Bigfoot.

"No," said one of the J.Crew brothers. "Make her stay. We need to keep an eye on her."

"How about an eyetooth?" said a different brother, licking his chops.

His friends howled with laughter.

Melody gripped Jackson's arm to steady herself. He turned on his fan and cooled his face.

"Stop!" Frankie sparked. "Melody is not the enemy, okay? Bekka is."

"Then they're working together!"

"We're not!" insisted Melody, lips quivering.

"Prove it!"

"Yeah! Prove it!"

Frankie clapped her hands once. "Guys, it doesn't matter because —"

"I can prove it," Jackson interrupted.

"How?"

"Because Bekka is after me too," he said.

Melody gasped. *Is he trying to save me or get me killed?* Once they knew Bekka had found the clip of Jackson on her phone, they would string her up to the carousel and play that creepy music until her head exploded.

"*Ka*," snapped Cleo. "What do you have to do with this?"

"Bekka found a video of me turning into D.J. She's going to play it on the news if Mel —" He paused, suddenly realizing where this was heading. "If I don't tell her where Frankie is hiding."

"How did she get it?" Cleo pressed.

"How'd she get it?" he stammered. "Um..."

Omigod. Omigod. Omigod. I need to be brave. I need to come clean. I can't be afraid. I have to tell them. I'm going to...

"My phone," blurted Jackson. "I dropped it at the dance, and Bekka found it."

Melody's shoulders relaxed back into their sockets. *Did he really just do that for me?* She squeezed her thanks to Jackson. *You're welcome*, he squeezed back.

"Fine. Case closed. Moving on." Cleo said. "Time to get back to our normal lives."

"How are we supposed to do that?" Billy asked. "There's a massive monster hunt going on out there."

Cleo exhaled sharply. Her bangs did the wave and then settled. "I dunno. Frankie, can't your father take you apart and then put you back together when this whole thing blows over?"

Her friends snickered into their palms.

"And what about me?" Jackson asked, fanning his face. "Who's gonna take me apart?"

Nice one! Melody thought, squeezing his hand.

"I'll ask my staff if they can preserve you for a few years," Cleo suggested with a *what-could-be-easier-than-that?* shrug.

Her friends giggled again. Melody wanted to grab the beakers off the steel countertop and hurl them at their heads.

"No wonder you're the queen of de-Nile," Jackson scoffed.

Yes! Melody squeezed again.

Everyone cracked up.

Cleo fingered her gold hoop earrings with royal indifference.

"Guys!" Frankie finally interrupted. "It doesn't matter! None of this matters. Because I'm going to turn myself in."

There was an audible gasp.

"You're crazy!"

"Do your parents know?"

"Can I have your makeup?"

"It's suicide!"

"It's for the best. The police want *me*, not you," she explained like a true heroine. If it weren't for her sparking fingertips, no one would have known how nervous she was. "Bekka won't stop until she can pay me back for making out with Brett, so—"

"Woo-hoo," whisper-cheered the pretty girl with the furry scarf. "Go, Fran-kay!"

Cleo's friends began silently applauding Frankie and her lethal kiss. In a much-needed moment of levity, she stood on the operating table and curtsied.

"Stop!" Cleo shouted. "Nobody move! Hissette is gone!"

Everyone turned away from Frankie.

"My bracelet! The snake. She's loose!"

A frantic search began.

"Maybe this is a good time to get out of here," Melody muttered amid the chaos. Jackson nodded and reached for the window.

"Bail up on the ankle biter!" shouted the Australian, pointing at an aquarium and the snake that was slithering up the side of the tank.

Frankie jumped off the operating table. "Get it before it eats the Glitterati!"

"*It* is a *she*," Cleo hissed, running toward the snake.

Deuce hurried toward Hissette, cupped his hands, and grabbed her.

"Eyes closed, everyone!" Deuce announced.

Frankie quickly scooped up the five glittering rodents from their cage and kissed the tops of their heads.

Melody and Jackson forgot all about the window and did what they were told.

"It's safe. You can open them now," Deuce said.

He slipped the snake back up Cleo's arm while her friends looked on in envy. She kissed him sweetly on the cheek.

"That was a live snake?" Melody whispered to Jackson.

"Uh-huh," he grunted.

"And now it's made of stone?" she whispered again.

71

"Yep. I'm pretty sure Deuce did that with his eyes," Jackson mumbled behind his hand.

Melody nodded, finally understanding why Deuce had freaked out when she took off his sunglasses at the dance.

"Hey, Frankie, *now* do you understand?" Cleo called out so everyone could hear.

"Huh?"

"Inviting a normie here is like asking my snake to hang out with your mice."

"They're *rats*," Frankie insisted.

Cleo stomped her foot and pointed at Melody. "Well, so is *she*!"

Just then the lights snapped on. In a panic, everyone hurried out the window and raced for home without exchanging a single good-bye.

Running hand in hand with Jackson through the soggy, dark ravine, Melody should have been leaping over fallen logs and skipping over puddles. After all, Frankie was going to turn herself in! Bekka would destroy the video of Jackson! No more "tick...tick...tick" messages! It was over.

Still, her limbs were so heavy she could barely keep up. As in her dreams, where she was running but not moving, she couldn't seem to get ahead. Too weird for Beverly Hills. Too normal for Salem. Too weird for normies. Too normal for RADs.

Melody wanted to stop running. She wanted to collapse into a heap of slick leaves and stare up at the moonless sky. To allow the clouds to cover her until she disappeared. To surrender her dreams to the wind. But every time she dragged behind, Jackson pulled her forward, forcing her to keep going.

CHAPTER SEVEN
A WINDOW OF OPPORTUNITY

Frankie woke up with her face pressed against the glass of the Glitterati's cage. Not because they needed comforting. The threat of Hissette had worn off the moment Deuce zapped her back to stone. And the booming thunderstorm had stopped shortly after the power came back. So the glittery rats slept peacefully, packed together like sprinkle-covered doughnuts in a see-through takeout box. This time it was Frankie who needed comforting. Turning herself in meant she might never see her parents again. She'd never go to prom or college. She'd never drive a car or fly on an airplane. She'd never be the CEO of Sephora or vacation in the Bahamas. And worst of all, she would never have a stitch-melting kiss with D.J. like the one she'd had with Brett.

Yes, the decision to confess was a tad on the impulsive side. Driven by the overwhelming gratitude she felt when her friends sneaked over to show their support. But if they could risk their lives for her, shouldn't she risk hers for them? Especially since this monster hunt was her fault in the first place. And double especially since *her* risk would call off the cops and give the RADs their freedom again. That is, if they considered hiding their skin, fangs, fur, scales, snakes, sweat, and invisibility to be "freedom." Because Frankie certainly did not.

"You want irony?" she grumbled, returning the Glitterati's cage to the steel table beside her bed. "I was fighting for freedom. And now I have less than I started with. And it's only going to get worse."

Their pink noses twitched.

"Thanks." Frankie tried to smile. "I love you too."

"Who are you talking to?" her father asked, entering without knocking. It seemed as though "right to privacy" had been added to the growing list of things taken away from Frankie, right after eye contact, social interaction, parental interaction, a cell phone, high school, TV, music, a voltage wardrobe, Internet, bedroom accessories, vanilla-scented candles, and fresh air.

Frankie hid her new iPhone under her blankets. "The rats," she said. "It's been pretty lonely in here, you know."

Viktor didn't respond. Instead, he shuffled across the linoleum in his worn UGG slippers and white lab coat and gathered his tools.

"What are you doing?" Frankie asked. Had Cleo's suggestion about taking her apart until this whole thing blew over somehow seeped through the walls and into his subconscious while he was charging?

"Building a family dog," he said, plunking his tools down on the operating table.

Frankie quickly scooped up her blankets (and the contraband iPhone) and dumped them in the far corner by the window. It was sunny outside. There was hope.

"Voltage! I'll help," she offered.

"That's okay," he said to the pile of metal gadgets on the operating table. "I'd rather work alone today." He flicked on the Cyclops light, refusing to lift his heavy lids and look at her.

"I could dye the fur or something," she pressed. "How about pink with green hearts? How mint would that be?"

Viktor sighed loudly and then ran his hand through his hair.

"*Dad*," Frankie pleaded, tugging the coarse white sleeve of his lab coat. "Look at me."

Viveka entered with a steaming mug of coffee for her husband. "Your father needs to work alone today." Barefoot and wrapped in a black chenille robe, she looked like she had the flu. Her radiant skin had dulled. Her violet eyes were red. Her black hair was frizzy. She set the mug down gently beside her husband. Longing for a reminder of life as it was, Frankie leaned toward Viveka and inhaled, desperate for a whiff of her mother's gardenia body oil. But the sweet smell was gone.

"Why does he need to work *alone*?"

"Because tinkering helps relieve his stress," her mother explained, still looking down.

"Stress that I caused, right?"

Just like Viktor, Viveka's tired eyes searched the lab...the table...the tools...willing to land on anything but Frankie.

"*Right?*"

They looked down.

"*Right?*" She sparked. Her anguish echoed off the bare walls. Still her parents remained silent. "Just say something! Tell me how mad you are! Tell me how much trouble I caused! Tell me you don't love me anymore! Just. Say. Something!"

75

Fear and frustration fused and then twisted inside her to form a double helix of rage. It spiraled to the core of her being and shook her foundation. Unable to control herself any longer, Frankie swiped her arm across Viktor's tools, knocking them to the floor in a hailstorm of clattering noise.

Viktor stared. Viveka rubbed her forehead. Frankie sobbed.

Viveka finally looked her daughter in the eye. "How could you possibly think we don't love you, Frankie? We feel this way *because* we love you."

The much-needed connection sent a zip of energy through Frankie's core.

"There's just a lot at stake and…" She placed her hand on Viktor's. "We're scientists, and since there's no science to keeping you safe, we feel like we're in over our heads and—"

"Well, you don't have to worry about it anymore," Frankie said, smiling bravely. She picked up the scattered tools and piled them in front of her father. "I'm going to turn myself in."

"Absolutely not!" Viktor boomed, smashing his fist on the table. The pile rattled.

"Frankie, darling, what are you trying to prove?" Viveka asked, her icy eyes melting to water.

"I'm not trying to prove anything, Mom," Frankie insisted, gearing up for another speech on her quest for change and freedom. But she stopped herself for fear of sounding like Buffy in season seven. The once-cool slayer could have bored vampires to death with her self-righteous lectures. It was enough to make Frankie turn the DVDs into nail polish coasters. "I just want to do what's right."

"Your decision is noble," Viktor said, placing his palms on the table and looking at Frankie. "But if you really want to do the right thing, you'll stop and think before you act. Not just about yourself or your mission but about the people you could hurt along the way."

"That's just it," Frankie insisted. "Turning myself in would help everyone. It would put an end to this whole thing."

"But it wouldn't help you. It would put you in serious danger," Viktor said. "And that would hurt us."

This time Frankie looked away.

"I filled your brain with fifteen years of knowledge," Viktor continued. "What you do with it is up to you. But *please*, make safe choices. Turning yourself in may be noble, but it's not safe."

Viveka nodded in agreement. "How about we give your father some space to tinker? I bet by the time the dog is built, he'll—"

The frosted window blew open and then slammed shut.

"Mind if I interrupt?" asked a boy's voice.

"Billy?"

"Yeah," he answered shyly.

"Billy Phaidin?" Viktor asked, obviously acquainted with him from the RAD meetings.

"Yeah, um, hi, Mr. and Mrs. Stein." Billy picked up one of Frankie's sheets from the heap by the window and wrapped it around himself. "I'm over here." A burrito-like figure shuffled toward them. "I know it's wrong to sneak into someone's home. And I want you to know I would never do anything creepy or pervy."

Frankie giggled.

"I just didn't want to draw attention to the house by ringing

77

the bell and having you open the door to some invisible guy. But I had to speak to you," Billy explained. "All of you."

Viktor raised his thick eyebrows and glared expectantly.

"I know how to keep Frankie from turning herself in," Billy said.

Uh-oh.

"How did you know she was going to turn herself in?" Viveka asked.

"Um, I…"

"He must have come in through the window just as I was telling you," Frankie blurted.

"It's true," Billy said. "I kinda had a hard time wriggling in, so I was listening for a while. I gained a few pounds over the summer, especially in my thighs. You may not have noticed because this sheet is so slimming, but—"

Viktor scratched the back of his head. "Well, if you just heard us now, how did you come up with—"

"So, what's your plan?" Frankie asked quickly, shutting down the interrogation.

"Paint me green and dress me in a cute little outfit so everyone thinks I'm Frankie. I'll turn myself in, wash off the paint, and ditch the clothes. Then I'll be invisible again, and I can escape."

Frankie beamed. "You think my outfits are cute?"

"*Frankie!*" Viveka snapped. "This is serious."

Viktor folded his arms across his lab coat. "If the police think Frankie has escaped, won't they keep looking for her?"

"Not if I leave a bunch of bolts and seams behind too. They'll think she gave up and took herself apart," Billy said. "Then all Frankie has to do is get rid of the hairstreaks, wear her makeup, dress like a man again, and go back to Merston. The normies won't have a clue she's the one who made out with—I mean... according to them, Frankie Stein is just another normie-skinned student. Not the mysterious green monster who lost her head at the dance."

"Hmm." Viktor considered Billy's explanation.

Viveka sighed. "I don't know. What would your parents think? Everyone is already blaming us for exposing their kids to danger. It's not responsible."

"It's okay. They're cool with it. I already—"

Frankie elbowed the sheet burrito.

"I mean, you're right," Billy backpedaled. "I'll definitely get their permission first. But for the record, my dad let me sneak into the KFC kitchen to find out what the seven secret spices are. And my mom once had me shadow the treasurer of the PTA to see if she was stealing funds. So they're cool with this kind of thing if it's for a good cause."

"You would do all this for us?" Viveka asked.

"On one condition," Billy said.

"What?" Viktor asked.

"Let Frankie fight."

Frankie smiled. She knew exactly what he meant.

"Excuse me?"

Billy stepped closer to her parents.

"Frankie wants to change things. And she is the only person I've ever met who is brave enough to do it," he said. "I've been waiting for someone like her for a long time. We all have. Let her do it."

"This is a war that can't be won," Viktor said. "Trust me. Everyone has tried at one point or another. And we've all lost."

"With all due respect, sir, our parents have lost. We haven't," Billy said. "But we've grown up hearing your generation's horror stories, so we're afraid to take a stand. Until now. Until Frankie. At least let her try."

Viktor and Viveka sighed. Had they been holding a white flag of surrender, the force of their breath would have blown it away.

Frankie put her arm on Billy's shoulder and squeezed her appreciation. *Who knew he was so muscular?* She was really starting to adore this guy. Her parents were supposed to think of ways to save her. It was their job, not Billy's. And yet he kept doing it again and again.

"I could probably whip up a Frankie face in about two hours. I still have the mold," Viktor said.

"Ew, creepy!" Frankie shuddered.

"And you can borrow my bad-hair-day wig," Viveka offered.

"Am I that easy to replace?" Frankie asked, slightly offended.

"Not even close." Viktor walked around to the other side of the table and hugged his daughter. He smelled like coffee and relief. "That's why we're going to do this."

"So, it's okay?" Billy asked.

"As long as you keep us informed every step of the way," Viktor relented. "If you're going to 'fight,' you need to think things through and be patient because, I have to warn you, it's going to be a very long and exhausting battle."

"Voltage!" Frankie said, pulling them all in for a hug. "I won't let you down this time. I promise." Suddenly, she broke away and hurried toward the window.

"Where are you going?" her father asked.

"To get my phone. I have to text Melody and tell her the plan. She needs to take FrankiBilly to Bekka and—"

"Where did you get a phone?" Viveka asked.

Frankie stopped and turned to the sheet burrito with a megawatt smile. "It just appeared out of thin air."

For the first time in what felt like forever, her parents smiled back.

CHAPTER EIGHT
FRENEMY TERRITORY

Lying on the sandy island in her bedroom—one knee up, one arm dangling loosely over the Nile's gentle current—Cleo was enjoying a near-perfect Sunday. Warmed by the rays of the sun and fanned by the lazy sway of bulrushes, she let out a long sigh. Aside from the occasional splaying of her hand to let the cool red river ease through her fingers, it was the most she had moved in hours.

Everyone in the palace was napping off the headache caused by Deuce's stoning. But Cleo couldn't seem to banish hers. The cause? Having a normie at last night's RAD meeting. Especially a highly attractive one who had made out with Deuce and was besties with Bekka—the girl who just so happened to be the initiator of the current monster hunt. A monster hunt that had filled her community with fear, slapped a curfew on her date night, and moved her overprotective dad to cut cell communications to and from the palace.

Seriously, had Melodork put some kind of normie spell on everyone? She clearly had a mysterious hold on Jackson and Frankie. How else could she have gotten into the RADs' well-preserved and heavily guarded circle? Cleo intended to find out…later. Right now she had bigger falafel to fry.

Peeling back the side of her bronze triangle bikini top, she checked her tan line. The two shades of brown—dark and darker—told her she was ready. After days of melatonin-sucking rain, her exotic skin had reclaimed its preferred tone—latte, light on the milk. It was time. She had to model Aunt Nefertiti's jewelry collection for her friends within the hour. Any later and her color would start to fade.

After a speedy but thorough application of amber body oil, Cleo slipped on a sand-colored tube dress, stepped into strappy leather platforms, and rolled Hissette up her arm. Careful not to clomp too loudly, she sprinted on tiptoe through the palace and hurried out into the sun-filled afternoon.

Striding down the block with her iPhone lifted to the gods, Cleo summoned the return of her service bars. When she was halfway down the street, near Jackson's white cottage, a symphony of *bwoop*s alerted her that she was back in the game. She had seven text messages.

Thank Geb!

TO: Cleo
sept 27, 9:03 AM
DEUCE: DID UR DAD LOOSEN UP YET? HOW'S HIS HEAD?

TO: Cleo
sept 27, 9:37 AM
CLAWDEEN: DID U GET HOME OKAY? ME & BROS MADE IT JUST BEFORE DAD WOKE UP TO PROWL. PHEW. SO MUCH TO DISCUSS. MELODORK, FRANKIE'S SURRENDER, HISSETTE ALMOST EATING RATS. LMAO! WANNA HANG? SOMEWHERE

SHADY. I NEED A WAX. ☹ BTW DIDN'T GET UR TEXT LAST
NIGHT UNTIL LATER. WHAT'S WITH THE JEWELS? SHOW ME.
OH, AND LOVE THE SIGN-OFF. #######

TO: Cleo
sept 27, 10:11 AM
LALA: JUST SAW UR TEXT FROM LAST NIGHT. DYING TO SEE
THE GOODS. WHAT R U DOING NOW? UNCLE VLAD SAID I
LOOK PALE. BEGGING ME TO EAT STEAK. SAID THE *V* IN
VAMPIRE DOESN'T STAND FOR VEGETABLES, THEN CRACKED
UP AT HIS OWN DUMB JOKE. GOING TO HEALTH IS WEALTH 4
IRON SUPPLEMENTS. WANNA COME? ALSO MUST DISCUSS
LAST NIGHT. FRANKIE IS GOING TO CONFESS. SHOCKING
(PUN INTENDED). ::::::::::::::::::

TO: Cleo
sept 27, 10:16 AM
BLUE: GOT SPRUNG COMING HOME LAST NIGHT BY UNCLE.
THOUGHT I WAS UP TO SOMETHING SHONKY WHEN HE SAW
MY BED WAS EMPTY. HE WAS SPEWIN MAD TILL I SAID I WAS
OUTSIDE IN THE RAIN, SOAKING MY SCALES. TOLD HIM I
DIDN'T KNOW WHAT A CURFEW MEANT. THAT IT MUST BE AN
AMERICAN TERM. HE ATE IT LIKE A WOMBAT AT A SALAD BAR.
WHAT'S UP FOR TODAY? THINK FRANKIE IS GONNA GO
THROUGH WITH THE CONFESSION? I RECKON SHE MIGHT
PULL A YEWEY AND CHICKEN OUT. CAN'T WAIT TO SEE YOUR
SPARKLERS. THEY SOUND RIPPER. @@@@@@@@@

TO: Cleo
sept 27, 11:20 AM
LALA: BACK FROM HIW. WISH U CAME. THEY WERE GIVING
OUT FREE SAMPLES OF QUINOA ICE CREAM. YUM. HEADING
TO FRANKIE'S TO HEAR THE NEWS. SEE U THERE? :::::::::::::

Frankie's?

TO: Cleo
sept 27, 11:22 AM
BLUE: GOING TO MEET THE MOB AT FRANKIE'S. U COMING?
@@@@@@@

Frankie's??

TO: Cleo
sept 27, 11:23 AM
CLAWDEEN: WHERE U AT, KITTY CAT? SEE U AT FRANKIE'S?
WE'RE IN THE BACK. ########

FRANKIE'S?

Cleo had no idea what they were talking about. Double no idea how they knew something before she did. And triple no idea why Frankie hadn't included her. But each knock of her wooden heels against the deserted sidewalk of Radcliffe Way was bringing her closer to the answers.

With a toss of her black hair and a roll of her glistening shoulders, Cleo marched across the cul-de-sac and rounded the side of the L-shaped fortress with mustered confidence. A tangle of electrical wires formed a barrier between the outside world and the dense rectangle of tall hedges inside. Creeping along the grassy perimeter, she listened for whispering voices, but the crashing sound of water drowned out everything else. *Now what?*

Another text *bwoop*ed at just the right time.

CLAWDEEN: CRAWL UNDER THE WIRES AND THROUGH THE
BUSHY THINGS. NOT AS THICK AS THEY LOOK. ########

Cleo did what she was told and emerged on a pristine flagstone
path. The cascading sound grew louder as she followed the walk-
way through the leafy maze.

"*Holy mother of Isis,*" she mumbled when she reached the end.

A wide horseshoe-shaped waterfall gushed over a fifteen-foot
cliff and crashed violently into a pool of froth and bubbles. One dip
in that skin-ripping cauldron and Cleo would emerge pure bone.

Still, Blue lay above the falls, scaly legs outstretched on one of
the flat rocks, splashing happily in the rainbow-spotted mist
while the other girls lay on their bellies on the manicured lawn
to the right of the pool. Each one had a yellow towel. Each one
rested her chin in her hands. Each one was smiling contentedly.
They could have been posing for a painting titled *Still Life of
Moving On Without You.*

"What's up?" Cleo asked with fake easygoingness. At least she
was tanned. That always gave her confidence a boost.

Clawdeen sat up. "Just talking about my Sweet Sixteen party.
Invites are going out on Monday."

"I know," Cleo said. "I helped you address the envelopes,
remember?"

"Isn't this place cool?" Lala asked with hurried nervous-
ness. "It's a backup electricity generator. There are turbines
behind the rocks. The Steins use it so they don't attract attention
with high electricity bills. Come sit." She patted the grass and

fang-smiled freely. "It's also the perfect place to gossip, because no one can hear anything," she added, wrapping her ever-cold body in a towel.

Cleo remained standing.

"What are you doing here?" Frankie pushed herself up to sit. Her white hairstreaks were gone, and her skin was painted normie color again. Suddenly, Cleo felt like the green one.

"Better question." Cleo twirled Hissette. "What am I *not* doing here? Why did I have to hear about this little get-together from my friends?"

Clawdeen and Lala exchanged an uncomfortable glance and sat up too. Blue waved innocently from the top of the falls, her blond ponytail wagging happily. It was obvious she couldn't hear a word they were saying over the sounds of the crashing water.

Frankie smoothed her pale pink dress and looked up, shielding her eyes from the sun. "I had some good news about my whole, you know, confession thing, and I wanted to share it." She shrugged to show it was that simple.

"And...?" Cleo squinted, the corners of her eyes still deliciously crisp from their morning bake.

"And...and I didn't think you would be interested."

"Why *not*?" Cleo asked with a deepening squint.

"You were so against everything last night that I didn't think you'd care," Frankie said, not looking the least bit intimidated.

"Try me," Cleo hissed, lowering herself to sit on the edge of Clawdeen's towel.

They told her about the FrankiBilly plan with an annoying amount of excitement. It was clever, and she told them that. But seriously, how long did she have to feign interest before she could tell them about her *Teen Vogue* shoot? Thirty seconds? Forty-five? Sixty? Anything longer than that and she would jump into the falls and hydroelectrocute herself...assuming such a thing was possible.

"Let's just hope Melody gets to Bekka before the deadline," Frankie said, checking the time on her iPhone.

"Melody?" Cleo snapped. "What does she have to do with this?"

"She's the one who's taking FrankiBilly to Bekka," Clawdeen explained. "Weren't you listening?"

"Yeah," Cleo lied. "I just don't understand why everyone trusts her."

Frankie, Clawdeen, and Lala stared at Cleo blankly. Blue splashed around happily in the distance.

"She's a *normie*!" Cleo pleaded with them. "They spread hate and propaganda with their sensationalized horror movies, trendy book series, degrading Halloween costumes, and corny school dance themes like Monster Mash." Cleo's eyes began to leak passion she didn't know she had.

"Melody isn't like the other normies," Lala insisted. "She's trying to help us."

"Stop being such a sucker, La. They're all the same. Normies have been exploiting my ancestors for centuries. FedExing our heirlooms to museums so that pretentious art lovers can ooh and aah about the ancient Egyptians and our incredible craftsmanship. Then, on their way out, they buy some King Tut coffee table book at the gift shop and complain that no one pays attention to

89

detail anymore. And it's total *ka*. They don't want incredible craftsmanship. They want Crate and Barrel. Because no matter what normies say in museums, they don't like different. I mean, *hello*? Have you watched *The Hills* boxed set? Frankie, your dad could build you a sister from the scraps their plastic surgeons toss. And guess who grew up in the Hills?"

The girls kept staring.

"*Melody!* Melody is from the Hills," Cleo continued, her voice cracking under the weight of her conviction.

"Actually, I'm not sure if Beverly Hills is actually 'the Hills,' " Lala said with the utmost respect. "I think the show is set in the Hollywood Hills. But it's confusing, I agree."

Cleo resisted the urge to yank the vamp's pink-streaked hair until she cried. "Well, wherever she's from, she turned Jackson against me. Did you hear what he said to me last night? He actually called me the queen of de-Nile. I mean, how unoriginal? Comebacks don't *get* more normie than that."

Frankie's iPhone *bwoop*ed.

The girls leaned closer to the screen, obviously grateful for the distraction.

"Melody and FrankiBilly are pulling up to Bekka's house now," Frankie reported.

They squealed with giddy anticipation. Cleo rolled her eyes. They were supposed to be squealing at her *Teen Vogue* news. Not Melodork's escapades.

"*Good luck,*" Frankie said aloud as she typed. "*Keep us posted.*"

She hit SEND, and the girls squealed again.

Minutes later, the update arrived.

"*Bekka is at the hospital visiting Brett,*" Frankie read. "*Heading there now. Still tons of time to make the deadline. Should be okay. BTW, Billy is awesome.*"

"Don't you think one of us should go down to the hospital?" Cleo suggested. "Just in case she tries to double-cross us?"

"She's not going to double-cross us, okay?" Frankie sparked. Clawdeen and Lala lowered their eyes and picked nervously at the yellow threads on their towels.

"Oh, really?" Cleo leaned back on her arms and lifted her face to the sun. "And who's the queen of denial now?"

CHAPTER NINE
CAN VERSUS MAN

California sunshine had finally found Oregon, and its intoxicating effect was hard to deny. Everything Candace drove past
buzzed with life—rain-spotted cars, hand-holding pedestrians, the
gauzy silver needles of Douglas firs. Not even Bekka's latest audio
threat could derail Melody's buoyant mood. She was minutes away
from saving Jackson and Frankie. Minutes away from showing Cleo
and the other RADs that she could be trusted. Minutes away from
taking action. And glorious weather had arrived to celebrate.

Ping!

Another text from Mom. It was the third one in the last hour.

TO: Melody
sept 27, 1:48 PM
MOM: IS BILLY IN HIS COSTUME? DID YOU FIND BEKKA YET?

Jackson's "full disclosure" policy with his mother had inspired
Melody to tell her parents the truth about her role in the local

scandal. It took some time to convince them that this whole "monster thingy" wasn't part of Salem's economic stimulus efforts but was, in fact, very real. Yet she had no regrets. As always, they told her how much they appreciated her truthfulness, and they vowed to keep her secret as long as she kept them informed. But three updates in an hour were a little excessive. So she simply replied STILL DRIVING and left it at that.

"NUDIs to the rescuuuuue!" Billy bellowed from the open moonroof of the Carvers' BMW.

A gaggle of mountain bikers turned their helmeted heads toward the forest-green SUV, apparently expecting some full-frontal exposure. Unfortunately for them, all they saw was Candace, dressed in designer camo, cracking up behind the wheel and high-fiving her new invisible best friend. It was the fifth time she had dared Billy to scream something out the window. But they laughed as if it were the first.

A sharp turn onto Oak Street propelled Melody from one side of the backseat to the other. But she wasn't about to criticize her sister's driving... or her sense of humor. Candace was the only member of NUDI with a license. And the clock *was* ticking.

"Hey." Candace turned to the empty passenger seat and slid her oversize white sunglasses up on top of her blond waves. Her green eyes filled with mischief. "Can I call you InvisiBilly?"

"Why are you looking over there?" Billy called from the third row. "I'm back here."

"No way!" Candace smacked the empty seat. "You invisible dudes are so fast!"

In the right lane, a guy driving a rusty pickup wiggled his

gold-ringed finger and pouted. "Taken," he mouthed, and then shrugged as if to say it was his loss.

Candace turned away. "Ew, guh-ross!"

"Stop flirting with married farmers," Billy teased.

"I *thought* I was talking to you," she giggled, turning toward the back.

"Hey," said Billy, quickly returning to the front seat. "I'm over here."

"I *love* it!" Candace shouted, blasting her horn.

Melody leaned forward and gripped her sister's shoulder. "*Can!*" she exclaimed, no longer concerned about offending her driver. "Stop honking. The hospital is a block away. We're in a quiet zone!"

"Then why are you screaming?" Candace whispered.

White news trucks—each with a satellite dish on its roof and a network logo on its side—were packed behind police tape like paparazzi banned from the red carpet.

"Are you sure this is the psychiatric ward?" Melody asked, shocked by the onslaught of people rushing toward the entrance. Few looked like concerned relatives. Most looked like reporters.

A computer printout of a hospital map floated above the front seat. "Building E," Billy confirmed.

"Yeah, *E* for *eensane*," Candace said, cruising up and down the rows of the bustling lot in search of a parking spot. A blond wearing an electric-blue blazer and a matching pencil skirt darted in front of the BMW gripping a microphone to her mouth. A camera-toting man hurried close behind. "I hope she's running to get her roots done."

"Are all these people really here because of Brett?" Melody asked.

"Hey, InvisiBilly." Candace lowered the passenger-side window. "Why don't you ask that poorly dressed reporter what's going on."

"Love to," he said with an audible grin. "'Scuse me, miss?"

Candace stopped beside her. Melody sank in her seat.

"Can you please tell me what all the excitement is about?" Billy asked.

Lips firmly closed, Candace stared at the woman.

"Um…" The reporter, unsure of where to look, searched the tan interior of the SUV. "That boy who saw the monster is coming out of shock. Doctors think he's going to speak."

"A million thanks, sweetheart," Billy said in a bass-deep tone.

The woman's light eyebrows shot up in terror. "What's going on here?"

"Are you hearing voices?" Candace asked sweetly.

The woman nodded.

Candace hit the gas. "Looks like you've come to the right place," she called, cackling as she sped away.

"You guys!" Melody giggled. She couldn't deny the humor, but practical jokes weren't exactly the best way to improve the RADs' public image. "I thought the NUDI goal was to show normies they have nothing to be afraid of."

"You're right," Billy said. "I'll stop."

"Fun *out*," Candace grumbled.

Melody buried her fists inside the long sleeves of her striped T-shirt and furrowed her brow. Had Candace and Billy just listened to her?

After ten more minutes of nearly running over reporters and gliding past rows of parked cars, Candace ditched the BMW in a spot reserved for Dr. Nguyen. It was either that or park in the lobby.

"Let's go!" Melody grabbed her khaki backpack and led the NUDIs toward Building E. The video of Jackson was minutes away from destruction. She could practically smell the waxy pastel crayons on his fingers as he held her face and kissed her thank-you. The promise of that kiss made her pink Converse rev.

It wasn't difficult for two attractive girls to flirt their way past reporters, student vigils, and the cell phone paparazzi. The two beefy security guards on either side of the sliding glass doors, however, didn't seem quite as charmed.

"Hang back. Let me handle this," Candace whispered in Melody's ear. "I have a way with bouncers."

"Candace, no!" Melody called, but it was too late. Her sister was already approaching the man on the left.

"Is she always like this?" Billy whispered in Melody's ear. She just nodded in exasperation.

"Press pass or visitor's pass," the security guard grumbled, adjusting the curly wire dangling from his earpiece.

"Really?" Melody nibbled her cuticle. This was the psychiatric ward of a hospital, not the *Vanity Fair* Oscar party. Although she imagined that the two venues weren't much different.

"Actually, sir, I was hoping you could make an exception."

Candace removed her white sunglasses and smiled with her entire body. Her sleeveless camouflage jumpsuit took the *fat* out of *fatigues* and gave her the silhouette of a short Victoria's Secret model. "You see, I really need—"

The human meatball raised his palm to silence her. "Hold on," he barked, pressing his sausage finger against the earbud and lowering his eyes as he listened. Candace turned to the other security guard, but his palm was lifted too.

Melody continued nibbling her cuticle. What if they couldn't get in? What if Bekka didn't come out? What if she missed the deadline? What if—?

"Maybe you should just give Billy the bag and let him go in alone," Candace whispered while the meatball listened to… well, whatever they were listening to. "He *is* invisible."

"Yeah, but the bag isn't!" Melody snapped.

"It's not like anyone will notice," Candace pointed out. "It *is* the psych ward."

"You already used that joke on the reporter. Now can you please be serious? This isn't a game—"

"Sorry 'bout that," said the security guard, fixing his attention on Candace. His hardened expression cracked, and out came a grin. It was a transformation Melody had seen a thousand times and had dubbed "Can versus man." Can always won.

"Hey, Garreth," he said to the guard on his left, "isn't this the cute girl you saw driving around looking for a parking spot before?"

"Might be." Garreth nodded. "Were you driving that green Beemer?"

"Yup," Candace smiled proudly. "It's diesel, you know. Good for the environment."

"Nice." He smiled. "Can I see some ID?"

"With pleaz-sha." Candace turned and winked at Melody as she searched her metallic bronze tote. "Here you go."

He looked at her California driver's license and handed it over to his partner.

"Candace Carver?" asked the guy on the right.

She nodded proudly. "The first."

"So you're not Dr. Nguyen?"

"Huh? No, who's that?"

"We got her," he said into his mouthpiece.

"You have three minutes to remove yourself and your diesel from this lot, or we will have you towed."

Melody lowered her head in her hands.

"Two minutes," insisted the meatball.

"But you don't understand," Candace pleaded. "We have to get into the hospital."

"Wait." The guard turned to Melody. "You're together?"

Melody shot her sister a soap opera–style *leave-now-or-I-will-destroy-you* glare.

"Candace *out*," she said quickly, and hurried off.

"No, we're not together," Melody lied. "I'm, uh, here to interview for the job." Billy coughed, and Melody jabbed her elbow into the air next to her. She heard a tiny *oof*!

"What job?" he asked.

"He's waking up!" someone—*a reporter?*—shouted from a third-floor window.

The crowd that was keeping vigil cheered. The camera lights flicked on. A stampede of reporters rushed the doors.

"Stand back, people!" called the guard on the right.

"You have your hands full, so I'm just gonna go," Melody told him.

And for some strange reason, he let her pass with a dismissive wave of his hand.

Managing to outrun the press tsunami by mere seconds, Melody and Billy raced up the dim stairwell to the third floor.

"Is this going to work?" she asked, panting, as the reality (or, rather, the risk) of what they were about to do set in. If they succeeded, this monster hunt would be over, and life would return to normal. But if they failed, Jackson, Frankie, and now Billy too would be in grave danger. And Cleo would be right—Melody would be to blame.

"You're not getting cold feet, are you?" Billy asked.

"Nah, just blisters," she lied, taking the last flight of stairs two at a time.

They burst onto the bustling third floor and ducked into the nearest ladies' room to prep FrankiBilly.

"Let me know if you need any help," Melody said, sliding her bag under the stall door.

"We're going live in five," someone shouted in the hallway.

"Live in five!" other voices echoed, spreading the word.

Minutes later, Billy emerged looking green and gorgeous in Grandma Stein's lace wedding dress. Melody couldn't believe how much he looked like Frankie had at the dance. They were even the same height. Aside from the sharp Adam's apple in his thin neck, he *was* Frankie.

"Let's wait until they're taping," Melody suggested. "That way everyone will see that the mysterious green monster has been captured, and this whole thing will be over fast."

"Sounds good," he said, checking the firmness of his self-adhesive neck bolts.

"Really? Are you sure about this?"

Billy nodded.

Melody put her arm around his surprisingly well-defined shoulders and smiled at the reflection in the mirror: a green monster and a dark-haired beauty. This is what she and Frankie would look like as real friends. Out together, standing side by side, in a public bathroom.

"Definitely worth fighting for," he said as if reading her mind.

Melody agreed and then fired off a quick text.

TO: Frankie
sept 27, 2:36 PM
MELODY: TURN ON THE NEWS. WE'RE LIVE IN 5.

Melody smiled to herself as she pulled open the bathroom door. After years of asthma and social persecution, she was starting to use her voice again.

And people were going to listen.

CHAPTER TEN

DON'T HATE ME BECAUSE
I'M BOO-TIFUL

A high-def shot of a drowsy boy lying in a hospital bed popped on the Steins' flat screen. Scrolling text along the bottom read: BRETT REDDING IS REGAINING CONSCIOUSNESS AFTER A SHOCKING MONSTER ENCOUNTER...FAMILY AND FRIENDS ARE STANDING BY, WAITING FOR HIS FIRST WORDS.

"Ahhhh!"

A five-way squeal, nearly powerful enough to spin the steel blades on the ceiling fan, rose up from the putty-colored L-shaped couch and filled the living room.

"Well, I'll be stuffed!" Blue slammed the cap on her tea tree moisturizer and rested her legs on Lala's lap. "He looks like a parade float with all those flowers around him."

"Normies can be so dramatic," Cleo said, admiring her pedicure from the comfy corner seat.

"Yum. Look at that platter of cold cuts," Clawdeen said.

"Ew," Lala winced.

"Are you *fur* real?" Clawdeen teased. "What a waste of fangs you are. You know what you should be doing with your teeth?" She turned toward Blue and pretended to bite her shoulder. "Paying a little visit to the Outback Steakhouse."

"Down, girl!" The Aussie chucked her bottle of tea tree lotion at Clawdeen, who howled with laughter.

"You wanna talk waste?" Lala shivered, wrapping herself in a black cashmere scarf. "What you wax off in one day would keep me warm for an entire year."

"Harsh!" Giggling, Clawdeen whipped the bottle at Lala.

"What about Jordin Sparks over there?" Lala whipped the lotion at Frankie's butt. It landed on the rug with a thud. "She wastes Vegas amounts of electricity."

"Nice one!" Cleo slapped her a high five. "The vampire strikes back!"

Everyone cracked up—except Frankie. She stood in front of the TV transfixed by the sight of Brett tucked under a blue-and-brown plaid comforter. His Neutrogena-clear skin was the ideal backdrop for his bloodred mouth, denim-blue eyes, and spiked black hair—a white canvas for the vibrant colors of his face.

Frankie's lips tingled. Her heart space swelled. It was the first time she'd seen Brett since their ill-fated kiss—a kiss that had ripped off her head, landed him in the psych ward, and threatened the future of Salem's RADs. The very sight of him should have filled her with fear. Shame. Anger. But instead her insides buzzed with longing.

D.J. who?

"Did we miss it?" Viktor asked, hurrying in with his wife. The tangy smells of sweat and metal wafted from his lab coat. The scents of gardenia and waxy makeup wafted from hers.

"Where's Billy?" Viveka asked.

"Shhh," Frankie hissed, standing before the TV with zombie-like deference. "Brett's regaining consciousness. He's gonna speak."

The camera shot widened to reveal the hospital room. Lemon-yellow walls were covered in get-well cards. A window offered a view of the parking lot. And Bekka—who stood next to Brett's mother—was wearing a WHITE IS THE NEW GREEN tee and a hopeful expression.

Frankie gasped. "How offensive is that shirt?"

"How offensive is her face?" Cleo said.

"Fur real," Clawdeen agreed.

"I'm glad Grandma Stein isn't around to see those tacky imitation hairstreaks," Viveka said to her husband.

"Shhh," Frankie insisted as the camera zoomed in on Brett. His beautiful lips were beginning to move.

A reporter hovered at Brett's bedside with a microphone and squinty concern. "It appears as if Brett is trying to speak," the man said in a deep voice that clashed with his boyish features. His name—ROSS HEALY—appeared at the bottom of the screen. "B-man, can you hear me?" he asked.

"Whashe," Brett mumbled.

Bekka and Brett's mother leaned closer.

"B-boy, can you hear me? It's Ross. Ross Healy from Channel Two News—you know, 'It's all true on Twoooo,'" he sang.

"Whashe," Brett mumbled again.

"He said 'Mommy'!" Mrs. Redding sobbed joyfully, her black chin-length curls bobbing for joy. "Did you say 'Mommy,' sweetie?"

"I've got your mummy right here." Clawdeen lifted Cleo's hand.

The girls giggled.

"Whashe!"

"He said, 'Where is she?'" Bekka explained, elbowing Brett's mother aside. "He wants *me*. He's looking for me." She twisted the top of his hair, spiking it up even more. "Aren't you looking for me, Brett?"

"Get outta there, ya crazy Sheila!" Blue shouted at the TV. "He wants Frankie. Not you, ya shonky yobbo!"

"Bekka?" Brett managed, and then coughed weakly.

A nurse hurried over with a beige cup of ice chips. Brett filled his mouth and reached for his girlfriend's hand. The instant their hands touched, his face brightened. Hers beamed. Frankie's dimmed.

"Are you okay?" he asked, his denim-blue eyes searching Bekka's hungrily.

Bekka nodded. "I am now."

A symphony of retching sounds burst forth from the L-couch. Frankie smiled on the inside.

"I was so worried about you," Bekka said, dabbing his wet lips with a tissue.

"Are you kidding?" Brett sat up. "I was worried about *you*."

"Isn't this amazing?" said Ross in a hushed voice, like some wildlife documentarian witnessing a giraffe birth. Frankie wanted to rip out her neck seams and strangle him. Now, *that* would be amazing.

"Bekka, I thought I killed you." Brett broke into a sob. A giant snot bubble burst from his nose.

"Aw, chunder!" Blue shouted. "Did you see that bush oyster?"

Bekka's beaming grin sank faster than a time-lapse sunset. "What do you mean, you thought you killed *me*?"

"Everyone, stand back," ordered a young male doctor with the word INTERN on the back of his scrubs. He rushed to Brett's side with a loaded syringe. "He's experiencing a post-traumatic hallucination."

"*What?*" Brett pushed the intern away. "I'm not hallucinating!"

"Yes, he is," Bekka insisted.

The intern stepped forward.

"I'm not."

The intern stepped back.

"He is."

The intern stepped forward.

"Let him speak!" Mrs. Redding shouted.

Everyone stepped back.

Brett tossed another ice chip into his mouth and turned to his mother. "Remember my tenth birthday party?"

She nodded tearfully. "We made a haunted house in the basement. You wanted a scary cake, so I baked a stick figure and we stabbed it with plastic knives and then topped it with a cherry compote drizzle."

"Yeah...well..." Brett scraped a chip of black nail polish off his thumb. "When I blew out the candles, I wished that..." He scraped some more. "I wished that I would..."

Scrape. Scrape. Scrape.

"It's okay, B-man," Ross whispered. "No one is here to judge you."

Brett took a deep breath. "I wished that I would turn into a *monster*." He exhaled. "And I *did*, Mom. I *did*!"

The intern stepped forward again. Mrs. Redding pushed him aside.

"Good gosh, Brett. Don't even *joke*!" his mother cried. "You're not a *monster*."

"How can you say that when I ripped my own girlfriend's head off?"

"*What?*" Viktor and Viveka cried out at the same time.

"Golden!" Cleo laughed. "He thought Frankie was Bekka!"

"They *were* in the same costume," Clawdeen pointed out.

"This is great!" Lala said. "You're off the hook!"

Frankie managed a convincing smile, because technically Lala was right. This *was* great. If Brett had no idea she existed, how could she possibly be blamed? His ignorance was a gift! A blessing! A get-out-of-jail-free card!

Then why does it hurt more than getting my head ripped off?

Different feelings rose and fell inside Frankie like painted horses on a carousel: relief, embarrassment, vindication, gratitude, melancholy, freedom, loss....But the one feeling that remained constant—the carriage seat that was bolted to the wood and didn't budge—was *insignificance*.

"You think that was *my* head?" Bekka asked.

Brett nodded.

"*My* head?"

"Yes!" He shouted at his hands. "I'm pure darkness!"

"*Brett!*" his mother gasped. "Don't *ever*—"

"It's true, Mom. Only someone truly twisted would try to kill a girl during the best kiss of his life."

Did he just say the best—

"Ahhhh!" The girls jumped off the couch and raced for Frankie. They hugged and squealed as if she had just won *American Idol.*

"Settle down," Viktor boomed. "This is my little girl he's talking about."

Viveka comforted him with a loving shoulder squeeze.

"*That* was the best kiss of your life?" Bekka asked, her green eyes sad and blue.

"Of course." Brett chuckled. "Come on. Admit it. You felt it too."

"Turn off the cameras!" Bekka screamed so loudly that her freckles quaked.

"Absolutely," Ross said, winking at his camera operator. "Okay, they're off. Continue."

"Brett, that wasn't *me*!"

"Yes, it was. I'm not crazy, you know," he insisted. "I was Frankenstein and you were my bride. I remember everything."

Frankie stepped closer to the TV. Her friends followed.

"Brett, that wasn't *me!* It was a monster. A real monster."

He laughed. "Who's the crazy one now?"

"It was me!" said FrankiBilly, barging into the room dressed as Grandma Stein on her wedding day.

The entire city of Salem gasped at the same time.

Brett's face brightened. Frankie's beamed. Bekka's dimmed.

"VOLTAGE!" Frankie jumped up and down, applauding. Raucous cheering and applause filled the Steins' living room.

"Fang-tastic!" Lala laughed. "He looks so much like you, Frankie!"

"What is this?" Bekka stammered—one part suspicious, two parts scared. "What's going on?"

"Brett, it's me," FrankiBilly said, walking toward him slowly. "I'm the one you kissed."

A pack of security guards burst into the room.

"Wait! Leave her alone!" they heard Melody shout in the background. "She's harmless!"

Much to everyone's surprise, the guards backed off.

"Who *are* you?" Brett asked.

"I'm the one responsible for all of this." FrankiBilly gestured to Brett's hospital bed and then to the mass of reporters and other people below his window. "And I want you to know that I'm sorry. I'll never go near you, or anyone else, again. I didn't mean to frighten—"

"Frighten?" Brett kicked off his plaid comforter and sat up straight. He was wearing his Frankenstein T-shirt—the one he'd worn on the first day of school. "I was afraid, but not of *you*. Of myself! I was afraid I killed you. Did I? I mean, did I hurt you? Because I didn't mean to. One minute I was having the best kiss of my life, and the next I—"

"Help!" Bekka yelled. "Somebody help him! That *thing* has taken over his mind!"

"Don't hate me because I'm boo-tiful," FrankiBilly said to Bekka.

"Oh no, he didn't!" Lala cracked up, high-fiving the other girls.

The security team moved in. This time, Ross and his crew held them back.

"VOLTAGE!" Frankie shouted. "This is just like watching *Gossip Girl*. Only it's real. And about *me*!"

"Melody did it!" Lala tossed her black scarf in the air.

Cleo rolled her eyes. "We'll see. It's not over yet."

Brett stepped toward FrankiBilly. "Nothing has taken over my mind, Bekka. Just my heart."

"It has his heart!" Bekka yelled. But no one cared what she had to say. Not when Brett was reaching for FrankiBilly's hand. FrankiBilly gave it to him.

"Are they going to kiss?" Clawdeen gasped.

Bekka lunged toward Billy. "Get away from him!"

Two security guards raced toward her.

"Put me down!" She thrashed as they took hold of her. "That thing is a monster! This town is full of monsters! They're stealing our men!" The guards lifted her by the armpits and carried her toward the exit. "Wait!" Bekka slammed her feet on either side of the doorway. "I have proof. I can prove it. I can prove it right now."

"Put her down," Ross insisted.

"Send in my friend Haylee," Bekka insisted.

Seconds later, her mousy best friend *click-clack*ed into the room with the unstoppable drive of a tightly wound toy. She wore a fitted tweed blazer, baggy slacks, a newsboy cap, and her signature beige cat-eye glasses. The only thing that kept her from looking so five decades ago was the iPad in the outer pocket of her green faux crocodile-skin attaché case.

Bekka wiggled her fingers impatiently. "Give it."

Haylee smacked the iPad into Bekka's open hand.

Frankie tugged her neck seams. "What is she doing?"

Bekka tapped the screen a few times, held it up to the cameras, and pressed PLAY.

"No!" Frankie shouted at the TV. "You can't do that! Melody got there way before the deadline! You promised!"

Viktor and Viveka gasped.

Blue scratched. Lala shivered. Clawdeen growled.

"See?" Cleo grinned as the video of Jackson Jekyll turning into D.J. Hyde began to roll. "I told you normies couldn't be trusted."

CHAPTER ELEVEN
ALL'S FAIR IN LOVE AND GORE

A swarm of reporters buzzed through the open door. Handheld microphones and suspended booms aimed for Bekka, eager to get a quote from the girl at the center of the story they had already dubbed the Salem Snitch Trials. But if it were up to Melody, *snitch* would be replaced with a more appropriate word for the freckle-faced female dog.

"Let me through!" shouted Melody, pushing past them.

Surprisingly, they did. But it was too late. The condemning video of Jackson had just been broadcast on Channel 2 and was being picked up by the national affiliates. Next stop: YouTube. Final destination? The world.

"What are you doing?" Melody grabbed the iPad right out of Bekka's clammy hands. "We had a deal! I gave you what you wanted."

"Oh, really? Because *that*"—she pointed at Brett and Franki-Billy, now seated on the edge of the bed and chatting softly—"was not part of the *deal*."

Haylee rifled through her attaché. "And I have the documentation to prove it."

"So, now Jackson has to pay for something Brett is doing?" Melody clenched her fists. "That makes no sense —"

"Excuse me, Miss Madden?" called a reporter. "Can you tell us about the boy in this video?"

Anxious for the scoop, the media descended on Bekka like pigeons on a pizza crust.

"Yes," she answered, happy to help.

"Are there others?"

"I'm sure of it. These freaks must have families."

"Have you received any threats?"

"If stealing the love of my life isn't a threat, I don't know what is."

"Back to the boy in the video. Is this split-wit capable of killing?"

Melody backed away from the feeding frenzy — whipped, beaten, and pureed. The evidence of her failure was immediate. Jackson had become the new Frankie faster than she could text I'M SORRY. "The Girl Who Lost Her Head" was old news. Everyone wanted the "Split-Wit" now. Not that they'd find him. Jackson was probably boarding a flight to London, fanning his sweaty face, and ruing the day he had met Melody Carver by the Riverfront carousel. Never knowing how deeply she would mourn his absence. Mourn the experiences they could have shared. Mourn the good they could have done. Mourn the voice she might have had. Death by media was quick and painful.

If only Candace had been there. She would have done something to distract the reporters. Something to pull the attention away from Jackson and put it on—

Wait! Melody's heart quickened. Her decoy was sitting beside Brett wearing a wedding dress.

"Excuse me for interrupting," she said, pulling Billy to his feet. "Did you paint your entire body or just the parts we can see?" she whispered into his wig. It had the sweet plastic smell of Barbie hair.

"Just the parts you can see," he said softly. "Why?"

"Take off your clothes. Become floating limbs. Give them something new to chase."

"Love it!" Billy snickered.

A minute later, Grandma Stein's wedding dress was lying in a lacy heap on the hospital floor. Two mint-green arms, Frankie's fake head, and the nape of Billy's neck were all that remained.

"Trick or treat!" he yelled, jangling about like a floppy skeleton.

Shrieks and gasps filled the crowded room. The medical staff bolted for the exit.

"Catch me if you can!" Billy called, leading the story-starved reporters down the hall of Salem Hospital's psych ward.

"Wait! What's your name?" Brett called. "Where are you going?" He began to chase after FrankiBilly, but Mrs. Redding insisted on going in his stead so that he could rest.

Bekka grabbed Mrs. Redding by her rose-colored cardigan. "You're seriously going to bring that *thing* back to him?"

"Mom, hurry!" Brett called. "They might hurt her."

Mrs. Redding took off in a sprint. Bekka followed her,

shouting something about getting stuck with grandchildren the color of algae.

Once everyone had left, Melody scooped up the lace dress and began smoothing out the creases. Mint-green makeup streaked the sides.

"Is she going to be okay?" Brett asked, his blue eyes moist with genuine concern.

Melody nodded with quiet confidence.

Brett stood up anyway. He wobbled slightly and gripped the bed rails to steady himself. "I'm going to check. Just in case."

Melody hurried to his side and eased him back onto the bed. "I think maybe you should stay here until you get a little stronger."

He strained to see what was going on in the hallway. "But what if they hurt her?"

"Trust me." Melody grinned. "He'll be fine."

"*He?*" Brett asked, looking shocked all over again.

"I mean—" Melody searched his face and then sighed. *Hasn't the poor guy been through enough? Isn't it time he knows the truth?* "That wasn't the girl you kissed," she whispered in his ear.

"Aw, come on!" He shot up. "Is everyone trying to mess with me, or what?"

"No one is messing with you, Brett. I promise. We're just trying to keep everyone safe. So that was a decoy. To keep Bekka from exposing the real girl."

"Who's the real girl?"

"I can't tell you that without her permission. But I'll ask her if she wants to meet you."

"Really? Does she go to our school?"

Melody zipped her lips.

"Just tell me this: Is she a real monster?"

Melody hesitated. What was she supposed to say now? She studied his eyes in search of a clue. They were wide with hope. Moist with tenderness. Hungry for the truth. Finally, she nodded.

Brett's rigid features softened to let her in. His smile was wide at first, but it soon fell to a frown.

"What's wrong?"

He sighed, lowering his gaze to his black fingernails. "I guess this means I'm *not* a monster."

Melody grinned. In some ways they were very similar. Darkness swirled beneath their shiny exteriors. They didn't want what other shiny people wanted. They were attracted to the twisted. Like human equivalents of San Francisco—there were unpredictable faults under their beauty. Their lives were an endless search for a safe place to stand.

"Why don't you become a NUDI?"

"A what?"

"It's my pro-monster organization. Normies Uncool with Discriminating Idiots."

He grinned. "Where do I sign up?"

"You just did."

"Sorry, Melody," he said sadly.

"For what?"

"For Bekka. I know you guys were friends. And Jackson's a cool guy. She shouldn't have done that."

"Thanks," Melody said, resting her forehead against the soundproof window. "Omigod, look!" she said, pressing her finger against the glass.

Below, cameramen were practically moshing as they fought for a shot of something on the pavement. Melody could see Haylee and Brett's friend Heath off to one side, but the mob was so thick that she couldn't see what had attracted the reporters' attention.

Brett grabbed the remote and flicked on the small wall-mounted TV. The screen showed a tight shot of Frankie's fake face lying on the curb of the parking lot. Nearby were the black-and-white-streaked wig and a stack of paper towels covered in mint-green makeup. Ross, slightly relieved but mostly disappointed, reported that the whole monster episode was a practical joke executed by a group of students at Merston High. Then he tossed back to the studio, where a special-effects expert was standing by, ready to speculate on how the crafty kids might have pulled off the prank.

Brett muted the TV. "It wasn't a prank, though, right?"

"I promise, she's real. I can introduce you tomorrow."

He smiled sweetly. His sincerity made Melody miss Jackson.

Minutes later, Ross Healy and his team returned to pack up their gear.

"You had me," he said, punching Brett with a fake one-two to the stomach.

"I had nothing to do with it," Brett assured him. "The joke was on me."

"Brilliant, B-man." Ross handed him a card. "Lemme know when something else goes down at that freaky school of yours. I'll hook you up with Gaga tickets or something."

Brett raised his thick eyebrows. "You think maybe I could shoot for you one day? I'm into filmmaking."

"Who are your influences?" Ross asked.

Confident that Brett wouldn't spill any secrets, Melody took her cue to leave and sneaked out to find Billy and Candace.

Outside the hospital room, a police officer was pressing Bekka for information about her involvement in the prank. "Miss," he said, smacking his leather notebook against his palm, "the more you cooperate, the lighter your sentence will be."

"*Sentence?*"

He nodded.

"I'm telling you, it wasn't a prank." She sniffled. "These monsters are real. Where's Haylee? Can someone find Haylee?"

"I saw her outside talking to Heath," Melody said, happy to deliver the bad news.

Bekka huffed. "Fine. Then ask her. She'll tell you. I'm not lying!"

The police officer eyed Melody with suspicion. "Do you know this girl?"

"I do," Melody responded respectfully. After giving her name and address to the police officer, Melody told him she was happy to help in any way she could.

"Oh, thank the Lord!" Bekka began sobbing.

"To the best of your knowledge, can you see any reason why Bekka..." He checked his notebook. "...Bekka Madden would have cause to believe she saw a monster?"

Bekka widened her green eyes in a desperate plea for mercy. Her look seemed to say "I'm sorry for everything"—the dissolved friendship, the blackmail, the phone threats, the broken promise, playing the video of Jackson....

Melody pursed her lips and considered the apology. Now that the hunt was over and life for the RADs would return to normal,

Melody actually felt sorry for Bekka. Brett was smitten with Frankie. Bekka had made a public fool of herself. And Haylee was her only friend. Wasn't that punishment enough? Did she really need to be arrested too?

"Bekka is an amazing girl. She would never lie," Melody stated.

Bekka stopped sobbing immediately. "See? I told you!"

"But a practical joke isn't the same as telling a *lie*, is it? I mean, if you ask me, it shouldn't be. Because what Bekka pulled off was more like art." Melody smacked her playfully on the back. "Just think about the amount of work that went into filming that video. Not to mention making the whole Frankenstein costume, organizing the special effects, and getting the police and the media involved. It's kind of impressive if you think about it. If there was an awards show for practical jokes, Bekka, my friend, you would clean up."

"What? You're lying!" Bekka turned to the policeman. "She's *lying*!"

"What's going to happen to her, Officer? Nothing *too* serious, I hope. She was just trying to be funny."

He adjusted his cap. "A healthy dose of community service, for starters."

Melody nodded in approval and then strolled off with a smug grin. She had just done her community a service as well. And it felt fantastic.

CHAPTER TWELVE
EAT, DRINK, AND BE WARY

Nothing against the Olympics. They're inspiring, and they originated in Greece, just like Deucey. But whenever they rolled around, Cleo's favorite TV shows were taken off the air and replaced with—and let's be honest—two weeks' worth of obscure, unendorsable physical activities. During that time, Cleo would often find herself wandering aimlessly around the palace like a lost camel in the desert, in search of something familiar to ground her. It was a disorienting, unnerving condition for which the only cures were the closing ceremonies and the subsequent return of her regularly scheduled programming. Once order had been restored, she'd celebrate by eating one of Hasina's decadent chocolate pyramid cupcakes, to replenish the inevitable calorie loss she'd suffered during her fourteen days of wandering.

And now, seated in the Allergy-Free Zone of the Merston High cafeteria with her three best friends, Cleo bit off the chocolate point of the pyramid in celebration of a different kind of restoration: the restoration of her regularly scheduled *life*. The one in which Clawdeen, Lala, and Blue focused on her like a high-performance zoom lens. The one in which newbies (*Frankie!*) and normies (*Melody!*) weren't making headlines. The one in which there was cell service in the palace. And dates with D on Saturday nights. The one in which she'd announce her *Teen Vogue* shoot, and her friends would sweat envy for days. The one that she was about to get back.

So far nothing pointed to the contrary. The cafeteria was filling up with hungry normies en route to their usual tables in the Peanut-Free, Gluten-Free, Lactose-Free, and new Fat-Free food zones. As usual, girls passed Cleo and her friends with a sideways glance to check their fashion-forward outfits. If Deuce wasn't around—and he wasn't on Mondays because of basketball practice—guys would do the same. They'd bop their heads to the lunchtime playlist, which today began with "I Made It (Cash Money Heroes)" by Kevin Rudolf. The lyrics couldn't have been more appropriate.

I've known it all my life
I made it, I made it!

Cleo chewed the rich pyramid-shaped cake to the triumphant beat that signaled her return. And with calculated patience, she flipped through photos on her iPhone, waiting for someone to ask the inevitable question.

"My Sweet Sixteen invites went out today," Clawdeen announced, biting her double bacon burger. "I kissed each envelope with MAC Girl About Town lipstick before I dropped it into the mailbox, which is why I was late for math this morning." She paused, obviously hoping for a reaction. Cleo refused—she hadn't been the center of attention in days, and it was starting to dull the shine on her hair.

Finally Lala leaned closer and peeked at the screen with her deep brown eyes. "Hey!" She flicked a dab of chocolate icing off the pyramid with her cold finger. It landed on Cleo's black mesh sweater and fell onto her pink-and-gray tie-dyed leggings. "What are you looking at?"

"Um, my stained pants!"

"Seriously, Sheila, whatever's on that celly must be ace, 'cause you haven't even noticed Lala's smudged eyeliner," Blue said, playfully tapping her gray-gloved fingers against her cheek.

"Nice. Make fun of the blind girl." Lala tossed salt on Blue's dry skin.

"You're not *blind*," Blue pointed out. "You just can't see your reflection."

"That's a good thing." Clawdeen twisted an amber curl around her long finger.

"No." Lala wiped her eyelids with a wet napkin. "It'd be a good thing if I couldn't smell your burger breath." She pursed her lips to avoid smiling in public.

Cleo, however, smiled out loud. Everything was back to normal. It was time.

"I'm trying to decide what to model for the *Teen Vogue* shoot," she said, as if they had been talking about it all morning. "I love the falcon necklace and the pear earrings, but wearing both together feels like overkill, you know?"

The girls knit their eyebrows in confusion. This scene couldn't have played out any better if she had scripted it. Which she kind of had.

Cleo swiped through the iPhone lookbook she had photographed earlier that morning. At dawn to be specific, when the sunlight was at its richest. The orange glow woke the gold the way kohl woke her blue eyes. She shot the priceless pieces on the sandy island in her bedroom and framed them with bulrushes and wild grass. Forget Cairo couture—her collection was pharaoh fabulous!

"What do you guys think?" She showed them photos of the earrings and the collar necklace. "Too much?"

"I think you'd better pause and rewind." Blue twisted her blond curls off her face and secured them with a pair of aqua-lacquered chopsticks.

"Fur real," Clawdeen said. "Those pear earrings are even better than—"

"Angelina's Oscar emeralds, I know."

Lala leaned across the table, the ends of her pink-and-black-streaked hair dusting the top of Cleo's pyramid cupcake. "Is there more?"

"Tons."

Cleo showed them the hammered cuffs, the stone-covered crown, the glow-in-the-dark ring, the feather necklace, and the ruby-eyed snake cuff—plus a beautifully lit shot of Anna Wintour's business card.

"Is it legit?" Lala asked, touching the screen.

"Of course! My dad found it in Aunt Nefertiti's tomb."

"No," Lala said. "The card!"

Cleo waved the girls closer. Once they were inside her amber-scented circle, she told them about her father's first-class encounter with Anna, the *Teen Vogue* shoot, the sand dunes, the camels,

124

her upcoming modeling debut, and the limitless networking potential. Their eyes widened with each new detail.

"Rack off, Sheila! You serious?"

"I would eat meat to be in *Teen Vogue*."

"I would go vegetarian!"

Intrigue had them wrapped around her like fine linen strips.

"Will you actually be on the camel?"

"Who are the other models?"

"Do they need any blonds?"

And banded them together with Herve Leger suction.

"Can we see the collection after school?"

"We'll help you pick the best pieces."

"Hey, mate, can we try anything on?"

By the grace of Geb, Cleo's image as queen, *their* queen, had been preserved for at least another day or two. *Crisis averted.*

She could have gone on for hours, and they would have listened. But her chocolate chip pyramid, which had happened to be at the center of their huddle, rose off its plate and began disappearing in bite-size chunks.

"Billy!"

The last bite fell to the plate. "Sorry."

Laughter blew the amber-scented circle wide open to reveal Frankie, Melody, and Jackson. They slid their white trays onto the rectangular table and sat as though they'd been invited. Which they hadn't been—at least, not by Cleo.

"Hey!" Frankie beamed through a thick coating of normie-colored makeup. Her tiny frame was enveloped in a scarf and a black satin jumpsuit (which looked more like a flight suit). Cinching it at the waist with a thick woven belt was an admirable attempt to put some Cover Girl in her cover-up. But it wasn't working. The one-piece garment had been made with the wrong kind of runway in mind.

"It's so voltage being back," she said, appreciating the hustle and bustle of the lunchtime crowd and bobbing her head as the song switched to Lady Gaga's "Alejandro."

Cleo rolled her eyes, unable to decide what bothered her more: the word *voltage*, Frankie's constant spotlight-jacking, or both. "The dance was Friday night," she pointed out. "It's Monday. You didn't even miss a day."

"I know." Frankie smiled. "Thanks to these two." She applauded Melody and the empty space beside her. Jackson, Lala, Clawdeen, and Blue joined in. Cleo pushed her cupcake aside. The celebration was over.

"I can't believe Bekka showed that video," Lala said to Jackson. "Were you freaking?"

"Pretty much." Jackson took off his black-framed glasses and cleaned the lenses on his crumpled brown-and-yellow-checked button-down. "I was running around looking for my passport when Melody texted me with the good news." He playfully pulled one of the strings on the normie's signature hoodie.

Cleo examined the new couple, wondering what Jackson saw in Melody. Feature for feature, she was undeniably attractive, maybe even super pretty. Long black hair, narrow gray eyes, a perfect nose, and zitless skin. But style-wise she had the whole Kristen Stewart *I'd-rather-be-comfy-than-cute* thing going on. Only she wasn't Kristen Stewart. So she looked like a pretty girl permanently stuck in Sunday mode.

"Billy was a real hero," Melody announced.

"The diversion tactic was your idea," he said, snatching up the discarded cupcake. "And you should hear how Melody stuck it to Bekka in the end. She has to do something like two hundred hours of community service."

"I heard about that." Clawdeen laughed. "Not bad. But if it were up to me, I would have had her sent to the electric chair."

"What's so bad about that?" Frankie joked.

Melody cracked up.

"Why are you even here?" Cleo blurted, no longer able to censor herself.

Melody blanched.

"Cleo!" Jackson snapped.

"I mean, um, don't you have allergies?" she backpedaled. "Shouldn't you be sitting in a different zone?"

"I have asthma, but it's been much better since I moved here," she said. "This morning I sang in the shower for the first time in years, and it actually sounded—"

"You sing?" Blue asked.

"You shower?" Cleo mumbled.

"Both." Melody said, ignoring the dig. "I used to perform when I was little. Why? Do you?"

"I play guitar," Blue said, "and a little piano."

"Still working on those scales?" Lala giggled into her napkin.

"Still working on those *jokes*?" Blue fired back.

Cleo continued flipping through the photos on her phone, hoping to reroute their attention back to what really mattered.

"Bekka got kicked out of math this morning and sent to Principal Weeks's office," Frankie announced with a snap of her electric-blue and black rhinestone-covered compact.

"Why?" everyone asked, shifting to face her.

"It was first period. And Mr. Cantor was late, so we started talking about the whole...*thing*. When Bekka came in, everyone started clapping and telling her how great the practical joke was. She tried to tell them it was real, but no one believed her. I guess she got so frustrated that she started whipping chalk around the room. And that's when Cantor came in. He took a piece of blue chalk right on the forehead. Sent her straight to Weeks."

"Nice," Clawdeen said, swiping a chicken strip from Jackson's plate.

"And her little friend too," Frankie continued.

"Haylee," everyone groaned.

"Yeah, Haylee. She tried to stick up for Bekka. Said she's upset because Brett wants a break but—"

"You know why he wants a break?" Melody interrupted.

They giggled and looked at Frankie. Frankie looked down at the table.

"That's ri-ight," Melody sang. "He wants to meet you."

The Allergy-Free Zone swelled with girly shrieks. Frankie sat on her hands. Jackson took cover from the female hormones by hiding under his floppy brown hair. Cleo wanted to hurl her phone at Melody's meddling face.

"It's true. He begged me to introduce you."

"That is so not safe!" Cleo snapped. "What if it's a trap?"

"Are you gonna do it?" Lala chomped on a carrot. "He is kinda cute for a normie...no offense, Melody."

She smiled to show there was none taken.

"I dunno." Frankie sighed. "What about D.J.?" she asked Jackson. "I think he likes me."

"I guess I could talk to him for you," he offered awkwardly from underneath his hair.

"So, is that a yes? Should I go and find Brett?"

"No, don't!" Frankie said. "Not here. Not in front of everyone. What if Cleo's right? What if it's not safe?"

"How about after school, then?" Melody suggested. "At the Riverfront. Jackson and I will go with you, just in case."

Frankie sighed again.

"Just say yes," Melody urged. "He really likes you."

"Fine. Yes."

The girls squealed with vicarious delight.

"Can we go too?" Lala asked.

"Yeah! We'll ride the carousel and pretend we don't know you," Blue added.

"Let's sneak out early or my brothers will follow us," Clawdeen said. "They don't think it's safe down there."

"Hold on! I thought we were going to look at the jewelry," Cleo said, unable to mask her disappointment.

"I know!" Blue, the peacekeeper, lifted a finger. "Why don't we do the Riverfront today and Cleo's tomorrow?"

"No way!" Cleo answered.

"Why not way?" Lala asked. She wasn't one for being told what she could and could not do.

"Because," Cleo said, stalling. "Because of the surprise."

"What surprise?"

"Um...I was going to tell you at my house but...Clawdeen

and Blue are going to be models with me," she blurted. "And Lala, I was going to have you help the stylists, since you don't really show up on camera too well, but—"

Another round of squeals filled the casserole-scented air. As usual, all the other students in the zone turned to see what they were missing. And as usual, Cleo grinned, loving the attention.

"But if you'd rather go to the Riverfront and chaperone, that's fine. I just need to know because I'd have to find replacements. Your call."

The girls assured her that replacements would not be necessary and that they were totally committed to the shoot.

"Golden," Cleo said, hoping to Geb that the editors at *Teen Vogue* would take the news with the same level of enthusiasm.

LOST CHAPTER
(WHOSE UNLUCKY NUMBER SHALL GO UNMENTIONED)

CHAPTER FOURTEEN
VANISHING ACT

It was the go-to topic of conversation in the lunch line and at parties, especially for the Wolf brothers.

"So, Billy, dude, be honest, how many times have you sneaked into the girls' locker room?"

"How hard would it be to get a camera in there?"

"Ever go to one of their sleepovers?"

"How about the locker room at Holy Oak High? Ever go in there?"

"The boys' school?"

"Yeah, to hear their basketball plays. Whadja think I meant?"

"No way, bro. He's too busy hiding out in the dressing rooms at Victoria's Secret."

Billy would pretend to laugh. But honestly? Billy didn't want to be *that guy*. The invisible horndog who followed hot girls and eavesdropped on their conversations. It was so predictable. Not to mention way slimy. Besides, only one girl captured his interest.

Captivating eyes. Fearless determination. Honesty. Innocence. The terrible outfits she had to wear to school and how she managed to smile anyway. The way her hands could light up a room.

He'd bought her a cell phone. Thrown a get-together at her house. And put his life in danger to save hers.

Now she was on her way to the Riverfront to meet a normie boy named Brett. Walking between Melody and Jackson. Sunshine warming her face. Her shadow trailing behind, giddy with the promise of new love.

Billy was following the shadow. Being *that guy*. The guy he didn't want to be. Each untraceable step brought him closer to knowing whether he'd ever have a chance with her. But something about her jittery fingers, her bouncy steps, her nervous laughter, told him that even if she knew he was there, even if he put on clothes and painted his face so she could see him, even if he declared his feelings on bended knee...he would still be invisible.

So he stopped walking and watched her go.

CHAPTER FIFTEEN
TO NORMIE IS TO LOVE ME

Honey-colored sunlight saturated Riverfront Park, empty-ing the last bits of lazy heat onto the grassy lawns and walkways. The weatherman had promised a beautiful day, but he had said nothing about the thick golden rays that seemed to track Frankie's face like a spotlight. That charged her from the outside in. That warmed her black hair and left the sweet smell of cherry-almond shampoo in her wake. No, he had said nothing about perfect weather for falling in love. Maybe he hadn't wanted to spoil the surprise.

"So, this is the infamous lucky bench?" she asked her escorts as they motioned for her to sit.

"Yup." Melody grinned. "This is where I met Jackson."

"I bet you weren't wearing a full-piece bodysuit, ten tons of makeup, and a scarf," Frankie said, wishing she could wear something a little more *her*.

"No, but I was," Jackson joked, offering her some of his popcorn.

"No thanks." Frankie rubbed her fluttering belly.

Organ music swelled, and the carousel began to spin. Bobbing up and down on their chosen horses, normie kids laughed and waved to their parents. And their parents waved back, eyes flooded with joy, moved by life's simplest pleasures. Children's laughter, a warm afternoon, the smell of popcorn in the air....If they only knew that their innocent landmark was the cork that topped the RADs' underground lair, built by monsters for monsters, because their world—the normie world—was too dangerous.

Frankie sighed, giving in to her own confusion. *What am I doing?* Her goal was to educate and enlighten the enemy, not to flirt with him. Not that Brett was the enemy himself, but he had *dated* the enemy. So his taste was questionable. "Remind me why I'm here?"

Melody grinned, waving at someone in the distance. "That's why," she murmured. Frankie turned. Brett was treading toward them in hiking boots. His swagger was deliberate—determined but not anxious.

"Right. Now I remember."

His jeans were the same navy blue as the Willamette River, and his black T-shirt had faded to comfy perfection. Green Ray-Bans concealed his eyes but not his megawatt smile.

Enemy who?

Away from the fluorescent lights of school, he looked different. Fresher. Boyish. Free. Out of his Frankenstein costume. No longer on TV. Without Bekka. He held a fistful of daisies in one hand and Frankie's cartwheeling heart in the other.

"Are those for me?" Jackson teased.

Frankie giggled quietly, not quite ready to be noticed.

136

"Hey," Brett greeted Jackson with a high five and an awkward chuckle. "How's it going?" he said to Melody with a *good-to-see-you-again* grin.

Everyone exchanged glances, unsure of who was supposed to do what next, while Frankie stood slightly off to the side and waited for her introduction...and waited...and waited....

But for some reason Melody and Jackson stared expectantly at Brett, like the next move was unquestionably his.

No longer able to handle the suspense, Frankie stuffed her sparking hands into her jumper pockets and then stepped forward.

"So," Brett asked, his eyes passing right over her. "Is she here?"

"Hey." Frankie smiled.

Brett looked at her, confused.

"It's me," Frankie pulled her scarf aside and quickly flashed a bolt. "See?"

Brett suddenly snapped to. "Oh, of course," he stammered. "You can't just walk around looking all—I didn't realize—it's you!" Brett finally made the connection between the girl in his geography class with the cool neck piercings and the hottie with the green skin who had rocked his lips. He was stunned into openmouthed silence.

"Should we get away from all these people?" Frankie asked, fearing he might faint and cause a scene. She had promised her parents she wouldn't do anything that would attract negative attention, and this time she intended to keep her promise.

"Sure," he said, trying to recover with an easygoing shrug.

They began walking toward the water.

"Oh!" He handed her the daisies. "These are for you."

"For what?"

"They're kind of a *sorry-I-ripped-your-head-off* gift."

Frankie pulled her hands out of her pockets and accepted the flowers with a genuine laugh, releasing an entire weekend's worth of tension, frustration, and shame into the breeze. From that moment on, their hands swung freely. Her fear of sparking vanished a little more each time their fingertips accidentally grazed.

Melody and Jackson followed them to a sunny patch of grass by the river.

"Man, I can't believe I'm hanging with some—" Brett paused and then sat. "Wait, what exactly are you guys?"

"We like to be called RADs," Jackson explained, snapping a dandelion from the ground and pulling its stem apart in strips like string cheese. "Regular Attribute Dodgers."

"Nice." Brett lay back and folded his hands behind his head. "So, are all of you RADs?"

"Not me," Melody said.

"That's right," Brett said, recalling. "You're a NUDI."

"A what?" Frankie giggled, fluffing her hair so he could catch a whiff of her cherry-almond shampoo.

"Normie Uncool with Discriminating Idiots," he recited proudly.

Melody applauded. "Nice memory."

"So, Jackson, that video of you was real?"

"Unfortunately." Jackson snapped another dandelion. "Something in my sweat triggers the transformation."

Frankie sat up. "Speaking of which, is it too hot for you over here?" she asked, suddenly afraid that D.J. would show up and crash their date.

"Don't worry. I'm cool." He tapped the mini fan in his blazer pocket. "Pun intended."

Frankie laughed at his corny joke, but only because she was happy. She lay down and stared up at the white streaks in the sky. "I totally remember the first time I saw you," she said to Brett.

Brett rolled onto his side and propped his head on his hand. "You do?"

Frankie nodded. "It was the first day of school. You and Bekka were talking behind me in the cafeteria line, and she said something about using a monster's butt as a pencil holder."

His cheeks reddened. "Oh, man, I remember that comment. It was so offensive." Brett took off his green Ray-Bans and began cleaning the lenses on his shirt.

"Why didn't you say anything to her?"

He studied her face with his denim-blue eyes while considering his answer. She sparked just a little.

He slid his glasses on. "Bekka is kind of fragile."

"Ha! If you think *she's* fragile, how would you describe *me*?" she joked, pointing at her neck seams.

He laughed. "I guess I was afraid to set her off."

Frankie rested her head on her hand, too, and then gazed out at the river. "Fear is boring."

He chuckled.

"What?"

"It's just funny, that's all."

"What's funny?"

"When I was younger, I wanted to be a monster so everyone would be afraid of me and I'd be afraid of nothing. And I was right. I mean, that's kind of how it works, isn't it? You're not afraid of anything, are you?"

Frankie thought about it and then shook her head.

"Wow."

"But it's not because I can scare normies. *Please!* They're much more dangerous than I am. I'm not afraid because, well, I've only been alive a couple of months, and I've been hidden away in my dad's lab for most of that time."

"So?"

"So, I'm too curious to be afraid."

Frankie scooted closer to his face and ran her fingers down his lenses.

"What are you doing?"

"It's like those smudges," she explained.

"What is?"

"Fear. It stops us from seeing clearly."

Brett took off his glasses and gazed at Frankie as though they were in a romantic movie—specifically, the part where the guy realizes he's falling in love.

"I wish you didn't have to wear all that makeup," he finally said. "Your green skin is so…"

"Mint?" She giggled.

"Yeah, mint."

She sighed. "I wish normies knew what we were really like."

Brett reached for her hand. She gave it to him. She rubbed her thumb over his black nail polish, wishing she had made time for a quick manicure.

"Omigod, hide!" shouted Melody. But it was too late.

"Freaks!" shouted a girl in the distance.

Frankie and Brett sat up with a start, then quickly lay down again as Melody shoved them into the grass.

"Bekka?" Brett mumbled at the sight of his ex-girlfriend. She was wearing an orange vest and dragging a giant trash bag through the park.

"Boyfriend-stealing zombie helpers!" she shouted at Melody and Jackson, stabbing a juice box with her wooden harpoon. "This is so not over!" A man in a matching vest ran over and quickly moved her to another section of the park.

Melody stood. "I don't think she got a good look at you. Let's get out of here before she realizes who you are."

No one argued. They hurried off in silence.

Once they reached Front Street, Brett finally spoke.

"I think I can help."

"I think she might need some space," Melody suggested politely.

"Not *Bekka*. The RADs." He pulled a business card out of his black leather wallet. "Remember that Ross Healy guy from Channel Two News?"

Melody nodded.

"He asked me look out for good stories around school. Maybe he can do something about you guys."

"Like what?" Frankie asked, secretly questioning his motives.

"A reality show?" Jackson said. "Like *The Secret Life of the American* Green*ager*?"

"No," Brett said with a laugh. "Something serious. More like a news piece, to show people what you're all about."

Frankie considered this. A news story would reach a lot of people. But was it safe?

"You should direct it," Melody said, knocking his arm the way guys do. "You've been trying to make a monster movie. Why not make it an exposé instead?"

"I dunno if I'm ready for something that big," Brett said

humbly. "Besides, it's not like Channel Two is just going to let some high schooler direct one of its shows. I'd be happy if they'd hire me to clean the camera lenses."

"It's safer than bringing an outsider on board," Jackson said.

"That's true," Brett admitted, wiping the smudge marks off his glasses and slipping them on again.

"I dunno, you guys," Frankie said, staring at the passing cars. Cars full of normies who were oblivious to the truth—a truth that would set the RADs free. But what if she messed up again? What if this exposé made things worse instead of better? What if someone got hurt? What if she didn't try? What would her parents want her to do?

"On one condition," she finally said.

They nodded expectantly.

"Everyone's face would have to be blurred. Our identities could never be revealed."

"I agree," Brett said.

"You can interview me first," Jackson said.

"I'll go second," Frankie said.

"I should probably call Ross before you get too excited," Brett warned.

"Too late!" Frankie beamed. "I really think this is exactly what we need."

"Me too." Brett smiled as though he might have been referring to something else.

Frankie smiled back, catching a glimpse of herself in his lenses. She may have looked goofy in her jumpsuit, but she felt beautiful in her skin.

TO: Frankie
sept 28, 6:18 PM
BRETT: ROSS LOVES IT! MUST HAVE CALLED ME B-MAN
50 TIMES. EVEN SAID I CAN DIRECT. SOMETHING ABOUT
IT BEING PRODUCED FROM TOP TO BOTTOM BY MH
STUDENTS MAKES IT MORE "ENDEARING." BUT WE HAVE
TO MOVE FAST. CAN U GET EVERYONE TOGETHER ASAP?

TO: RADs, Melody
sept 28, 6:21 PM
FRANKIE: VOLTAGE OPPORTUNITY TO BE ON TV AND
CHANGE THE WORLD! MEET IN MY BACKYARD AT 8 2NITE.
BLANKETS RECOMMENDED. DISCRETION REQUIRED.
SAFETY GUARANTEED. XXXXXXX

TO: Brett
sept 28, 6:21 PM
FRANKIE: 2NITE FAST ENOUGH FOR U? ☺ XXXXX

CHAPTER SIXTEEN
TEARS OF A CROWN

Candlelight flickered against the stone walls in Cleo's bedroom, providing a tomblike authenticity to her well-crafted jewelry display. Or, rather, the display she had asked the staff to create. She had texted Beb and Hasina while she tuned out a lecture on supply and demand during last-period economics class. But Mr. Virga would have been proud. Her text was supply and demand in its purest form. She had asked them to *supply* her with...

1. One hundred amber-scented candles

2. Three dry linen strips in a basket outside the bedroom

3. Polished stone floors

4. Raked sand on the island

5. Blue Egyptian water lilies floating in Nile

6. Three open sarcophagi outfitted with full-length mirrors

7. *Teen Vogue* playlist:

    a) "Poppin' " by Utada
    b) "Lisztomania" by Phoenix
    c) "Far From Home" by Basshunter
    d) "Your Love Is My Drug" by Ke$ha
    e) "Nobody" by the Wonder Girls
    f) "Rude Boy" by Rihanna

8. A veggie-and-hummus platter for Lala

9. Noncomedogenic dye-free moisturizer for Blue

10. Organic beef jerky for Clawdeen

11. Jewelry hung on a linen-covered board

12. A washing basin with Egyptian cotton hand towels

...and had *demanded* it all be done by the time she got home from school.

Now, amid the heady scent of amber and the rhythmic claps in Utada's song "Poppin'," Cleo elbow-guided her blindfolded friends through her flickering chamber. She positioned them in front of the white wrapped board that showcased her twinkling treasures. It stood proudly before the three open sarcophagi like a highly decorated queen facing her handmaidens.

"Rea-dy?" she asked in a singsong voice.

They nodded anxiously.

"Okay, take off your blindfolds!"

The girls pulled the linen strips off their eyes and dropped them onto the stone floor. Miu-Miu and Bastet padded over to claim their new toys and hurried off before the birds could steal them.

"Clee!" Clawdeen gasped. "They're even more amazing in real life."

"That's what he said." Cleo giggled.

"Can I touch?" Blue asked, whipping off her polka-dot gloves and reaching for the glow-in-the-dark moonstone ring.

"That's what he said," Lala blurted.

They all cracked up. But no one laughed harder than Lala, now free to let her freak fangs fly.

It was an old routine, something that brought them to giggle-tears back when they were in grade school. And it kept on delivering. The familiarity of it all put Cleo at ease. Her girls were back.

After washing their hands in the soapy basin, they reached for their favorite pieces and began trying them on. Lala crunched on celery sticks while fastening and unfastening the gold relics with the patience of a true stylist.

Without hesitation, Cleo lifted the jewel-encrusted crown and lowered it onto her head. The weight grounded her bare feet to the stone. Fused the tips of her black bangs to the tops of her lashes. Signified her position in the social hierarchy.

"*Fang-tastic*," Lala said, recording the look in a papyrus note-book. "I say no earrings. Just that long snake bracelet and you're done." She was so confident behind closed doors—vivacious, opinionated, and strong. A totally different Lala from the shy, sullen girl she was at school. And for a split second Cleo saw the value in living openly. Liberation was Windex for the soul. It let the light shine through. But why dwell? Nothing was ever going to change.

"I agree," Cleo said, admiring the completion of her first look in the mirrored sarcophagus.

"I'm all over these," Clawdeen said, holding the pear-shaped jade earrings up against her auburn curls.

"Add these and you're good," Lala said, handing her the hammered cuffs. "Oh, and make sure you wax your arms right before the shoot."

"I'll book Anya right now. What's the date?" Clawdeen asked, popping a piece of organic beef jerky into her mouth.

Cleo's stomach lurched. *Teen Vogue* didn't even know they existed yet. "Um, October fourteenth," she muttered, and then reached for her goblet of pomegranate iced tea.

"Morning or afternoon?"

"Evening."

"Will they be providing hair and makeup?"

"Of course."

"Wardrobe?"

"Yes."

"Dinner?"

"Yeah."

"Will they give us notes so we can take the day off from school?"

"I'm sure they would."

"What about transportation?"

"What about it?"

"To and from?"

"For the love of Isis! Stop talking so I can *think*," Cleo snapped, wondering how she could have possibly forgotten to confirm the girls.

"What's there to think about?" Clawdeen asked.

"Nothing. Sorry. I'm good." Cleo whipped out her phone, quickly deleted some annoying cry-for-attention text from Frankie, and fired off an emergency message to Manu.

TO: Manu
sept 28, 7:40 PM
CLEO: PLS CONTACT *TEEN VOGUE* ASAP. FORGET NORMIE MODELS. THEY NEED TO HIRE CLAWDEEN AND BLUE INSTEAD. LALA AS STYLIST ASSISTANT. NEED CONFIRMATION NOW. ^^^^^^^^^^^^

"What a beaut!" Blue called from somewhere in the room, her voice muffled.

"Where is she?" Cleo asked Lala and Clawdeen.

They shrugged, craning their necks.

All of a sudden, the sarcophagus in the far corner of the room opened with a slow creak. Blue stepped out admiring the moonstone ring.

"What were you doing in my armoire?" Cleo asked with a charmed grin.

"I wanted to see if the stone really glowed in the dark," Blue said. "And it does. It bloody well does! Like a giant pearly-pink clump of *tobiko*," she said, referencing the flying-fish eggs that hatched her brethren. "I'm wearing this one for sure."

Ping!

Cleo checked her phone. *Letitbegoodletitbegoodletitbegood...*

TO: Cleo
sept 28, 7:44 PM
MANU: EDITOR NEEDS TO SEE THEIR MODELING PORTFOLIOS AND COMP CARDS BEFORE BOOKING.

"Ugh!" Cleo pressed down harder on the crown and summoned the strength of her ancestors before responding. *What would Cleopatra VII do?*

TO: Manu
sept 28, 7:44 PM
CLEO: NO DEAL. TAKE IT OR LEAVE IT. MY JEWELS, MY RULES.

A pair of gray Egyptian nightjars flew out of Cleo's sleep loft to sip from the red muddy water of the Nile. If only they could appreciate how stress-free their lives were.

"You said the shoot was in the evening, right?" Clawdeen asked, pulling a Motorola Karma from her red leather crossbody bag.

Cleo nodded at the screen of her iPhone, willing Manu to hurry and text back some good news.

"Hi, Anya, it's Clawdeen. I'm going to be modeling for *Teen Vogue* and will need a full body wax the morning of October fourteenth." She checked her long striped nails. "And a nail art manicure too. Something Egyptian. Please call me back to confirm at—"

"See if they can fit me in for a hydrating treatment," Blue called.

"I'll take a steam," Lala said.

Clawdeen nodded and continued adding to the message.

Ping!

MANU: OKAY AS LONG AS THEY CAN PHOTOSHOP. THEY INSIST THAT THE GIRLS BE PROFESSIONAL. ANY MISHAPS AND THE SHOOT IS OFF.

"Yes!" shouted Cleo.

The Egyptian nightjars flapped back up to the sleep loft.

"Were you just reading Frankie's text too?" Blue waved her phone.

"Huh? What text?"

"About being on TV and changing the world."

Lala and Clawdeen checked their screens.

"We're blowing up!" Lala announced. "First magazines, now TV!"

"I reckon we should hire agents," Blue said.

Clawdeen hitched her purse over her shoulder. "I *reckon* we should get going. The meeting is in three minutes."

Blue slid on her gloves.

"Wait," Cleo said. "You're not leaving now, are you?"

"Why not?" Lala asked, pulling a violet cashmere turtleneck over her head.

"Because"—Cleo splayed her arms—"we're kind of in the middle of something here."

"We're done." Lala waved her notepad as proof. "I have everyone's looks. There's nothing left to do."

"What about pose practice? And squint-prevention exercises?"

"You're joking, right?" Clawdeen said flatly.

"No."

Flickering flames illuminated their blank stares.

"In case you forgot, we've never done this before. And if this shoot doesn't go well, they'll cancel the feature. Cairo couture will be out for another five thousand years, and my jewelry designs will never take off. This is my big chance."

Just saying those words made her stomach roil.

"I totally get it, Cleo," Blue said, hating to argue. "But what about *my* big chance?" She hung the moonstone ring back on its hook. "You have ace connections. But what do I have? I want to be a pro surfer. Who's going to sponsor a scaly girl in gloves?"

Lala snorted.

"Things need to change for us, Cleo," Blue said, scooping up some Nile water and rubbing it on the back of her neck. "Normies need to start accepting us, or we'll never land our dream jobs."

Cleo rolled her eyes.

"Aren't you tired of hiding? Don't you want to be normal?" Lala asked, spearing a couple of cherry tomatoes on her fangs.

Clawdeen laughed. "La, you couldn't be normal if you tried."

"There's nothing *special* about normal," Cleo insisted with a slight lift of her chin.

"Didn't it feel good to go to that dance dressed as our real selves?" Blue asked gently.

"It wasn't worth the price we paid, if that's what you're asking."

"What if there wasn't any price?" Clawdeen tried.

"There's always a price," Cleo said, shocked by her own cynicism. Was it change she opposed, or a changing of the guard?

"I wanted to be an exchange student because my parents told me it would be different in America," said Blue, suddenly very serious. "They said there was a bonzer RAD community here, and the RADs were going to change things. They wanted me to grow up better than they did. And ever since I got here, I haven't had the heart to tell them fair dinkum. My e-mails and postcards are full of bodgy lies." Blue walked to the door. "So I reckon we should give the Sheila a listen." Her cute duck walk suddenly seemed annoying to Cleo.

"After the trouble she got us into last time?"

"We're just going to listen," Lala said, following Blue. "Come on."

Clawdeen stood between them, fidgeting with the zipper on her purse, obviously torn. "We *should* work on our poses."

Cleo grinned approvingly. She could always count on Claw to have her back.

"Not to be a bludger, but we have two weeks for that." Blue placed her hand on the scarab doorknob. "And this meeting sounds important."

"More important than *Teen Vogue*?" Cleo stomped her foot, wondering when Blue had become so assertive.

Lala burst out laughing. No one else saw the humor, though. "Oh." She shivered. "I thought you were kidding."

"Thought wrong." Cleo folded her arms across her black mesh sweater and jutted out her hip. The sudden movement caused the crown on her head to tip forward, but she caught it before it fell. Unfortunately, the same could not be said about her social status. "Fine," she said with a defeated sigh. "I'll listen."

She hung up her royal jewels and followed her friends to Frankie's house, all the while silently swearing it would be the very last time.

CHAPTER SEVENTEEN
THE GHOUL NEXT DOOR

RADs emerged from the starlit maze of trees and marveled at the sight of the Steins' secret waterfall. Frankie welcomed each of them with a *thanks-for-coming* hug and offered those with blankets a seat on the mist-covered grass. Those without joined Melody on the stony ledge of the frothing pool. The tangy smell of dinner lingered on their clothes, and yet their eyes were full of hunger. But what were they craving? Change? Revenge? Their own MTV reality show? Melody flipped up the hood of her black sweatshirt and buried her hands in her sleeves. She'd know soon enough.

"Hey," she said warmly to a girl with white cat-eye glasses, red zipper earrings, and a mess of blue hair. "I'm Melody."

The girl emitted a groan that sort of sounded like *Juliaaaa*. Then she pulled a thick day planner from her tote and slowly, as if in a trance, crossed 8 PM MEETING off her three-page to-do list.

Others joined them on the ledge and whispered cautiously among themselves.

"Not bad for short notice, huh?" Jackson said, high-fiving Melody. His fingertips were smeared with green and yellow pastels. "And it was all your idea," he shouted over the sound of the pounding water.

Several heads turned when he said that. Once they saw he was referring to Melody, they turned away and began whispering.

"It was not," she insisted loudly. If this idea was a bust, she certainly didn't need the RADs knowing who to blame.

"Was so." He tossed back his floppy brown bangs. "What did you have for dessert tonight? Humble pie?"

Melody rolled her eyes at his corny grandpa humor "Ha-ha." She reached for his hand and quickly changed the subject. "Looks like you've been drawing."

"Just messing around." He leaned back, dipped his fingertips in the rushing water, and dried them on his jeans. "While you and Frankie were getting organized, Brett and I were working on graphics ideas and titles." He leaned close and whispered, "We're thinking of calling it 'The Ghoul Next Door.' What do you think?"

I think you give me heart-shaped goose bumps when you talk in my ear.

"I love it." Melody giggled.

"So does Ross." Jackson beamed.

Melody's insides inflated with joy. "Yesssss," she meant to shout. But it sounded more like singing. Clear, pure, beautiful singing. It was a sound she hadn't heard in years. Her elation was so uplifting that she leaned forward and hugged Jackson to keep from floating away.

"Get a tomb," someone snarled in passing.

Cleo!

Flanked by her friends, the queen bee-otch trolled for seats with a reluctant shuffle. Julia stood and offered Cleo her spot on the ledge. Without hesitation, Cleo took it. One after another, three spaces opened up, and her friends claimed them. Had they paid these girls to warm the stone until they arrived? Or were they just that intimidating? Like Melody had to ask. She'd spent her whole life warming stone for the popular girls in Beverly Hills. But seats never seemed worth fighting for. Nothing did… until now.

Suddenly, the falls stopped falling, and the remaining water gurgled out like a high-speed bathtub. Silence—sharp and jarring—hit the group like a smack.

"Much better." Frankie flashed a thumbs-up to her parents, who were standing at the back of the blanket-patched lawn with a remote control. They wanted to trust her. They said they did. But it was obvious from their tight grins and pained expressions that they weren't quite there yet. And that they were going to hang around to see what happened.

"What I have to say cannot be shouted," Frankie said softly.

Everyone scooted closer to hear.

"First, thanks for coming on such short notice." She sat and began swinging her legs over the wet cliff. She was still wearing her flight suit and makeup, but her scarf was gone. With every kick, the moon found her delicate neck bolts and kissed them with its cool white light. "Last week I tried to show the normies at school how voltage we are, and, well, we all know how that turned out."

Snickers swelled and then settled.

"But now, thanks to Melody, we have another chance."

Oh no.

"The normie?" chirped a gecko-faced boy seated on a bamboo mat. "Not again!"

"She's not a normie," Jackson snapped.

Huh?

"She's a NUDI!"

"Oh, I'm down with that," chirped Gecko Boy. He slapped his buddy five and then twisted his hand to separate their sticky palms.

More snickers. Viktor and Viveka exchanged glances.

"It means Normies Uncool with Discriminating Idiots," Billy said from somewhere. "And by the way, you're acting like a discriminating idiot if you don't give her a chance."

Melody beamed a thank-you smile from one side of the lawn to the other so Billy would see it from wherever he was.

"*Ka,*" Cleo said, coughing quickly.

Clawdeen elbowed her with a surprised giggle.

After years of sitting down, Melody finally stood.

Dozens of eyes fixed on her. Glowing in the darkness like bulbs on a Christmas tree—some green, some red, most yellow. They watched her expectantly, waiting for her to move them to a place they had never been before. Just like the audiences that used to wait for her to sing. Only this time, instead of drawing on a voice that had once come so easily, Melody was forced to use the one that never had. She was stepping into the spotlight to defend herself—a role she had never imagined choosing. And yet there she was, front and center.

"I get why you don't trust me," she began, shaking. "And I

guess if I were you, I'd have a hard time with it too. But I'm on your side. I thought I proved that when I took Billy to the hospital, but I guess it wasn't enough. So I'll keep trying." The more she spoke up, the lighter her lungs felt. Her voice became clearer, smoother, and silkier. Like oil in an unused car engine, it just needed to be turned on and used.

"Why do you care so much?" asked Cleo, sounding bored.

"Because I know how it feels to surrender a seat to someone who thinks she's better. I know how it feels to want 'normal' so badly you hide the qualities that make you special. Most of all, I know how it feels to change those things. And *that's* the most degrading feeling."

Julia, obviously moved by Melody's admission, nodded in agreement but lowered her head so sleepily that her glasses slipped off and fell to the ground. Embarrassed, she bent down, one vertebra at a time, picked them up, and then slowly backed into the darkness.

"So, please, trust me," Melody continued. "And when you stand up for yourselves, let me stand with you. So together we can—"

Everyone started applauding. Their shining eyes were moist with compassion; Melody's were moist with relief. *Was it really that easy?*

Smiling at Jackson, she sat and exhaled fifteen years' worth of angst into the starry sky.

Once the applause had faded, Frankie introduced the "voltage guy" who would help the RADs take their first steps toward standing. Brett Redding came out waving from the canopy of trees and was greeted with an audible gasp. He gasped back when he saw the illuminated eyes of his audience.

159

Frozen with awe, he addressed them from the back of the lawn. "Dude, this is so awesome," he murmured.

They spun around to face him.

"So..." He clapped his hands together nervously. "Um, I have some great news.... Wait, I should probably introduce myself. My name is Brett Redding—oh, you probably know that, since we go to the same school. I'm the guy who accidentally ripped Frankie's head off and then freaked, which you also probably know because it's been all over the news." He snickered.

They didn't.

"Anyway, while I was in the hospital, one of the news guys gave me his card and, well, long story short, Melody, Jackson, and Frankie thought it would be a good idea if I made a documentary about you so people would see how cool you are, and Ross, the reporter, agreed. So he's letting me direct it, and he's going to put in on Channel Two during the Spotlight on Oregon week. Any questions?"

Hands shot up. It looked like a mass audition for a deodorant commercial.

"Um, yes, you with the sunglasses."

"What's up, Brett?"

"Oh, hey, Deuce, I couldn't see you in the dark. What's up, man?"

"I was just wondering why you want to do this. It's not like you have anything to prove."

"This film combines my two favorite things in the world, movies and mons—I mean, RADs." He paused and looked up at Frankie. "And now that I'm getting to know you, I want to help."

"Cool," Deuce said, satisfied.

"That's it?" Cleo sounded aghast. "You're okay with that?"

"Yup," Deuce answered flatly.

"What do we have to do to be in it?" asked someone else.

"Agree to be interviewed. Share photos, stories, hopes, dreams..." explained Brett.

"Sounds dangerous," someone whispered.

"All of your faces will be blurred, so no one will know who you are. Your identities will be completely concealed. It's a first step toward showing people that you're harmless."

"Hey, mate, will our relatives all over the world be able to see it?" asked Blue.

"It's just airing locally for now. But I can burn copies for you if you want."

"Ace!"

The questions kept coming. "Where will you film it?"

"My shed. It's completely private."

"What's it gonna be called?"

" 'The Ghoul Next Door.' "

A burst of laughter said the crowd liked it.

"Will you do any audio-only interviews—you know, for those of us who don't show up on film?" asked Lala.

"Sure! I'll show other images while you're talking."

"Fang-tastic!"

"When does it air?"

"October fourteenth," Brett said. "Oh, and if you're going to be in the show, you have to be in the studio when it airs. They want you to answer questions from the viewers, live."

"Then everyone will know who they are," Viktor pointed out in his deep voice.

"I'll make sure those shots are blurred too. And...we'll get some security guards to keep the room private—no one will see you exit or enter."

Cleo stood. "Let's go," she said to her friends.

No one moved.

"You heard him." Cleo hitched her purse over her shoulder. "You have to be available on October fourteenth, and you're *not*. So let's *go*."

The three girls exchanged glances.

"I said let's go!" Cleo stomped. "This...*whatever*-it's-called is the same time as our *Tuh-een Vuh-ogue* photo shoot," she said, enunciating *Teen Vogue* in case the people in Portland couldn't hear her. "And I promised the magazine editors we'd be professional, so we have to pass."

The girls stood reluctantly.

"Wait!" Melody called, not wanting to lose the most dynamic girls in the group. "Can you change the date of your shoot?"

Cleo hate-squinted, crushing Melody between her fake lashes.

"Why don't you change the date of *your* shoot?"

"We can't. It has to air during the Spotlight on Oregon week. And since yours is only fashion, can't you—"

"It's not *only fashion*," Cleo spat. "It's about fashion *and* history. *My* history."

"Well, this documentary is about your *future*," Melody countered.

The RADs applauded again.

Cleo turned to face her detractors. "A future that none of you will have if you put it in the hands of normies!"

She whipped back around to find her friends seated again, their

162

elbows linked in solidarity. Melody actually felt a little bad for Cleo, but she was thrilled the girls were going to do the documentary.

"Really?" Cleo sneered at them. Then, without another word, she marched past Brett and disappeared behind the trees, leaving behind a trail of amber-scented rage.

Again Melody inhaled its bittersweet smell, and she wondered if her attempts to fit in were uniting this group or tearing it apart.

CHAPTER EIGHTEEN
QUEEN TAKES GREEN

The final bell *bwoop*ed. It was over. She'd survived.

Day three of school without friends was just like day two, which was exactly like day one. *Inconceivable!* Social extinction wasn't something Cleo had ever anticipated. What next? Clawdeen needing hair plugs? Lala buying steak knives? Blue summering in the Sahara? Now, faced with the unimaginable, she was forced to make the best of a bad situation and embrace the afterlife... or at least make everyone think she had.

Thank Geb for Deuce. He'd stuck to her like liquid resin. But after seventy-two hours of basketball recaps, sunglass shopping, gossip-free lunches, and noxious guy smells, Cleo was starting to unravel.

"My game starts in forty," he said, holding the double doors open with the flat of his Varvatos high-tops. "Wanna grab a slice first?"

Cleo saw herself in the lenses of his brown Carrera aviators. An overcast October sky behind her... a lackluster black

turtleneck...expressionless eyes. She sighed. Sports and slices—
is that what her life had become?

All around her, Merstonites spilled from the mustard-colored
building. Friends connecting like magnets, anxious to share the
details of their afternoon before racing home to text. It was the
loneliest part of her exile. The time she dreaded most.

"I don't get it," Cleo grumbled, just as she had for the past
seventy-two hours. "Why would anyone choose teen rogue over
Teen Vogue?"

"Their loss," Deuce said absently, slapping a fellow baller five
and promising to see him on the court in a few.

Cleo, pretending not to be irritated by the interruption, gripped
Deuce's elbow. Ready to begin a death-defying descent down the
school's front steps while teetering in three-inch python mules,
she asked, "You think they'll change their minds?"

"Can they?" he asked while nodding hello to another basketball buddy.

"They'd better. The shoot is thirteen days away."

"Wait, I thought they bailed."

"I haven't exactly told the editors about the whole 'bailed'
thing yet."

"*Nice.*" Deuce lifted his palm for a high five. "Who said mum-
mies don't have guts?"

Cleo lowered his hand. "I thought they would have come
crawling back by now."

Just then, Clawdeen, Blue, and Lala hurried by, giggling and
swinging their bags like it was the last day of classes. They could
have swung them right into Cleo's heart. It wouldn't have broken
any more.

"Maybe you should talk to them," Deuce said after they had walked across the campus in silence.

"And say *what*?" Cleo dropped his elbow. " 'Sorry for giving you a once-in-a-lifetime opportunity to wear Aunt Nefertiti's priceless collection'? Or 'Will you ever forgive me for getting you into a top magazine'? How about 'My bad for vouching that you'd be professional'!" she shouted, no longer caring whether Clawdeen's keen hearing picked up every sarcasm-soaked word.

"Yeah." Deuce adjusted his green-and-tan snowboarding hat. "Forget them. Let's just grab a slice."

Hurried footsteps closed in behind them.

"I think ve missed heem," said a disappointed girl.

"I knew we should have split up," slurred her friend. "What if Simona and Maddie found him first?"

"Vatever, ve're the ones in drama club. Ve'll nail this. *Ah-ah-ahhhh!*"

Cleo turned to see two ninth graders dressed in black unitards and capes. Their faces were pasty white, and their lips cherry red. If it hadn't been for their wax fangs, one might have thought they'd walked face-first into a wet painting of the Canadian flag.

Instead of following Deuce to the crosswalk, Cleo stopped. "Excuse me. Why are you dressed like that?"

The blond—who had obviously sprayed her hair black, because there was a yellow patch in the back—removed her fangs and leaned close to whisper, "Haven't you heard?" She smelled like aerosol and cherry-scented lip gloss.

Cleo lifted one eyebrow and shook her head.

"Brett Redding is casting for a reality show about monsters. It's being picked up by the CW."

"I heard Fox," said the naturally dark-haired vannabe.

"But you're not monsters," Cleo said, searching the thinning campus for a possible explanation.

"Yes, ve are." The vannabe vinked and then removed her fangs.

"It sounds like another practical joke," Cleo said, pretending not to notice Deuce waving her over. "How'd you hear about this?"

"Why? You wanna try out?" Blond Patch asked suspiciously.

"Just don't be a vampire," the brunette stated.

"How 'bout a pretty witch?" the blond suggested. "We saw a ton of witchy stuff in the costume closet. The drama room should still be unlocked if you want to take a look."

"Or an evil Barbie?" Natural Brown countered.

"Or the bogeyman." Blond Patch laughed.

"Omigod, *yes*!" Her friend cracked up. "You can hang bok choy from your nose."

"Bok choy? Why bok choy? That's so random!"

"I love saying it. Bok choy, bok choy, bok choy."

They cracked up.

Cleo glared. If her head could have spun any faster, she would have taken off like a helicopter. "How'd you hear about this show?"

Blond Patch reached inside her tan leather backpack and handed Cleo a crumpled flyer. "You know that girl in your grade...old-lady glasses and psycho tights...always trailing Brett's ex, texting?"

Cleo nodded. *Haylee!*

"She gave this to me during lunch."

ZOMBIES

took over

BRETT REDDING'S

MIND!

THEY FORCED HIM TO BREAK UP
WITH HIS GIRLFRIEND AND DIRECT A
MONSTER PROPAGANDA MOVIE

BOYCOTT OR
BE CAUGHT!
YOU DECIDE.

Meet at the flagpole
by the main doors to
organize and strategize.

3:15 PM THURSDAY,
OCTOBER 1

*COPIES OF FLYER PAID FOR BY
HUNT (HUMANS UNITE! NO TOLERANCE).

Cleo crumpled up the flyer. "This is just another practical joke. Trust me."

"Vhatever," said Blond Patch, reattaching her fangs. "Your losssss."

The girls hurried off in search of fame while Cleo tossed the flyer into the trash with a swish that would have impressed Deuce, had he seen it. Instead, he was leaning on a fire hydrant, with his back to her, thumb drumming to whatever song was blasting from his iPod.

Cleo yanked out his right earbud. "Ready."

"What was that all about?" Deuce asked, standing.

"Some normie freaks who want to be in Brett's movie," Cleo huffed. "I can't believe anyone wants to be in that thing."

"You mean normies, right?" he asked, impatiently pushing the button at the crosswalk a few times.

"No, I mean anyone," Cleo said. "It's suicide."

The walk signal flashed.

"I'm going to be in it," Deuce said as he stepped off the curb.

Cleo pulled him back by the collar of his leather jacket. "What? Why didn't you tell me?"

"I thought it was assumed."

"*Assumed?*" Insecurity slithered up through her belly and wrapped itself around her heart. "Why would I assume you'd be in the movie that's ruining my life? If I were going to *assume* anything, it would be that you'd be at *my* shoot for support. Not that you'd be helping the enemy!"

An elderly lady shuffled by. She eyed Cleo with contempt, probably wondering why such a nice young girl was standing on a public street corner causing a scene. Cleo crinkled her nose and stuck out her tongue at the nosy old bat. The woman looked away in horror. It didn't solve anything, but it felt good.

Deuce took her hand. "Cleo, I'm not the enemy, remember?"

"You are now!" she said, breaking free and hurrying off as fast as she could in her three-inch mules. Her heart sank with each tottering step. She was totally alone. But the pity party would have to wait. She needed a plan. Fast. She looked back toward the school.

The campus, breezy and gray with the promise of rain, was empty except for two hunched figures sitting cross-legged by the flagpole. *Aha!*

Purrrr-fect.

"Meetmearoundbackunderthebleachersacrossfromthesnack-machineifanyoneisthereignoreme," Cleo whispered to them as she passed. She stomped up the cement steps without looking back.

She made a show of opening her locker and stuffing her history text into her metallic gold tote, just in case Billy, the gossip, happened to be lurking. She listened for the sound of his breathing and checked the floor for Starburst wrappers. Nothing. Cleo hurried out the side door.

The back of Merston was a place Cleo rarely visited. As far as she was concerned, tracks were for finding runaway camels, and football was something you got from a stiff pair of sandals. But this was life-and-death critical. Exceptions had to be made.

Bekka and Haylee were already there when she arrived. After checking to make sure there weren't any lingering jocks, Cleo climbed the bleachers and sat directly above her marks. She opened her textbook, pretending to read about self-government in British North America. After another quick scan, she knocked her wooden heel against the aluminum tier.

"Can you hear me?" she mumbled. "One knock for yes."

Knock.

"Are you working alone?"

Knock.

"Who told you about this movie?" she whispered, wondering if the RADs had sprung a leak.

"Ross Healy. Channel Two," Bekka whispered back. "I was listed as a reference on Brett's film résumé. I said he was a great director, but that was before Ross told me about the zombie propaganda movie. God, why didn't I think to ask *before* I gave the reference? I feel like such a—"

Cleo knocked her heel. "There's no time for *feeling* anything. Just answer the questions." She turned a page in her textbook. "What's your objective?"

"First, to stop the spread of pro-monster propaganda by shutting down the movie. Second, to prove monsters live in Salem and bring them to justice. Third, to get Brett ba—"

Knock! "No feelings."

"Sorry."

Cleo considered this three-pronged plan carefully. Objective one was the same as hers. Shutting down the movie would have the girls begging for forgiveness and, more important, would get them recommitted to *Teen Vogue*. Then she would take Bekka down before she had time to say "objective two."

"You have a plan?"

Knock.

"Tell me."

"How do I know I can trust you?" Bekka asked, stealing the upper hand and slapping Cleo with it.

"I'm here, aren't I?" Cleo snapped.

"Not good enough," Bekka snapped back.

Cleo stuck her tongue out at the aluminum bench above Bekka's head. *Does this normie loser have any clue who she's dealing with?*

"You could be a spy," Bekka explained further.

"I am," Cleo blurted, thinking fast. "But I'm not working for them. I'm working against them. I've been watching them for years."

A whispered exchange passed between Bekka and Haylee. "Why?"

"I'm a zombie hater. Long story," Cleo said, feeling momentarily guilty for betraying Julia. But this was war. And if staying alive meant talking trash about the undead, so be it. She was doing it to protect them.

"Who is their leader? What do they want? What are their weaknesses?"

Cleo pressed her lips together. She wanted to sabotage the movie, not destroy her friends. The royal was loyal.

"Let us join your cause," Bekka pressed.

"Denied. I work alone."

"Then what good are you?"

"What good are *you*?" Cleo fired back.

"I know all of Brett's passwords. I'll log on to his computer and erase the movie before it airs."

Not bad.

"How are you going to break into his house?"

173

"He works at school. AV room."

Not bad at all.

"What can *you* offer?" Bekka asked.

"I can find out when the movie is done so you'll know when to erase it," Cleo tried.

More whispering.

"Fine," Bekka agreed, as though she was doing Cleo some massive favor. "Does this mean you want in?"

"Two conditions." Cleo turned another page in her history book. "One, no one can know I'm a member of HUNT. Agreed?"

"Why not?"

"Agreed?"

Knock.

"And two, you and Haylee have to stop writing that stupid cell phone novel about me."

"You know about *that*?" Haylee asked in her high-pitched voice.

Cleo stomped her heel. "You mean, *Bek and Better Than Ever: The True Story of One Girl's Return to Popularity After Another Girl Whose Name I Won't Mention—CLEO!—Hit on Brett Then Got Hit by Bekka Then Basically Told the Entire School That Bekka Was Violent and Should Be Avoided at All Costs?* Yeah, I know about it."

Whispers rose like smoke through the spaces between the tiers of the bleachers.

"Do we have a deal?" Cleo asked impatiently.

Knock.

"Good." Cleo stood and clomped down the bleachers. "I'll be in touch."

CHAPTER NINETEEN
THIRD-DEGREE BURNS

From the outside, Brett's backyard shed had less hang-appeal than a frayed bungee cord. Relegated to the far end of the square lawn—past the tree house, grill, and tetherball—it was the shy kid at the party watching everyone else have fun on the dance floor. Its worn cedar siding was masked by cobwebs, crusty leaves, overgrown weeds, and bird poo. The windows were streaked with mud. It was hardly the kind of place a gentleman took a lady on their first date. But Frankie was no ordinary lady. And this was no ordinary date.

"Here it is," said Brett, sliding open the shed door.

A pair of glowing red eyes flew toward them from the back of the shed and stopped dead in front of Frankie's face. If she hadn't seen the fake black rubber bat bobbing up and down on its zip line, she might have sparked until Thanksgiving.

"Cute," she said tickling its distended belly. She saw the words MADE IN CHINA stamped under its wing.

Brett smiled, relieved. "Bekka hated Radar," he said, shaking his head at the improbability of it all. "She hated everything about this place."

He lifted his arm to tug the pull chain that dangled from the bald red lightbulb. Frankie inhaled his pine-scented deodorant all the way down to her belly.

"Whaddaya think?" he asked amid the hellish glow.

Had there been a more fitting word than *voltage*, Frankie would have used it. Instead, she fell back onto his black futon and looked around in awestruck silence, allowing her wide eyes to say it all.

Shoulder-high stacks of classic horror VHS tapes had been glued to form pedestals, on which were displayed his favorite monster busts: Frankenstein, Dracula, Godzilla, Sasquatch, a zombie, a werewolf, the Loch Ness monster, and the headless horseman with a magazine cutout of Spencer Pratt taped to his neck. The walls were papered from top to bottom with vintage Frankenstein movie posters. Arranged chronologically and protected by high-gloss shellac, the artist renderings of Grandpa Stein made the shed feel more like a scrapbook than a scrap heap. More important, they assured Frankie that Brett didn't just accept her—he had been waiting for her.

"This is like a mini museum," she finally said.

"I've been collecting since I was seven," he said, sitting beside her. "It's weird, but if you think about it, I knew your family before you did."

Frankie angled her body to face him. Brett angled to face her. He rested his elbow on the back of the couch and allowed his hand to dangle alongside her chin. Black nail polish, a silver skull ring, and a green watch face set atop a thick leather cuff; it felt as if he'd been built just for her.

"You know what would look great in here?"

Brett shook his head.

"Grandma Stein's wedding dress."

"You mean the one you wore at the dance? That was—"

Frankie nodded. "Yup. The *real* bride of Frankenstein's," she said, charged with the promise of his excitement.

She held her smile, expecting him to gasp. Studied his denim-blue eyes waiting for that spark of recognition. Checked his blood-red lips anticipating a jaw drop. But Brett hardly moved at all. He just gazed at her through the jagged frame of his droopy after-school hair the way one might gaze at a beautiful sunset, with an expression frozen somewhere between admiration and gratitude.

Brett leaned toward her. Frankie lifted her face to meet his. If only she had been wearing that beautiful white lace wedding gown instead of a long-sleeved black-and-white seersucker dress... or maybe that hot-pink chiffon minidress on Bluefly.com. Or a peasant blouse and jean shorts, or a yellow off-the-shoulder tee and cropped jeans.... But all that would have to wait until the RAD revolution was won. Not that Brett seemed to mind. His lips were approaching hers with one thing in mind....

Frankie quickly checked her neck seams while every crackling watt of electricity inside her seemed to be pressing against the front of her body, pushing her closer to him. As if she needed pushing. Her eyelids closed, her lips parted, and her hands rested gently on his arms.

"Hey," said Heath Burns, barging in through the sliding door.

Frankie and Brett broke apart, currents of displaced desire undulating between them, unsure of where to go.

"Sorry I'm late," he said, dragging two six-foot-long light stands behind him.

Not late enough.

"No worries," Brett said, getting up to help his best-friend-slash-production-assistant. "Our first interview subject isn't here yet, so..."

"Cool." Wiping his forehead with the sleeve of his dark purple hoodie, the thin redhead sighed. "Where do you want this?"

The boys spent the next fifteen minutes transforming the shed into a film studio. They covered the fake-blood-smeared windows with black felt. Pulled the futon away from the wall to achieve depth. Slid Radar the bat back into his starting position. And moved all eight VHS pillars into the background of the shot.

Once everything was set, Heath powered up his lights. Their set snapped to life. "Dude, this is gonna be so insane," he said, admiring his work.

"You know this is top secret, right?" asked Frankie, even though Brett had assured her endlessly that his normie buddy could be trusted. "No one can know where we're shooting or who we're shooting. Ever."

"Why do you think I was so late?" Heath asked. "I was being stalked by half the drama department," he offered. "It looked like I was being chased down the street by a pack of vampires in some B movie."

"Man, I wish I'd been there." Brett chuckled. "How'dja ditch 'em?"

"I hopped on the public bus."

Brett laughed. "Where'd you take it?"

"Across the river. I had to take a cab back, or I would have been even later."

"Oh, man, that's classic." Brett high-fived his buddy and then turned to Frankie. "Trust him now?"

Frankie was about to apologize when someone knocked.

"Who is it?" Brett called.

"Jackson."

Heath slid the shed door open and welcomed the first subject inside. The sight of him weighted Frankie down with guilt. Somewhere behind his thick black glasses and swingy mop top, D.J. was waiting to come out. And when he did, he would expect to find Frankie, not Frankie and Brett.

But what was she supposed to do? Time-share her boyfriend with Melody? Advocate global warming? Deny her feelings to spare his? Thankfully, Jackson hadn't broken a sweat in almost a week, so it hadn't become an issue yet. But summer was only nine months away. She would have to tell D.J. the truth eventually.

"Killer space," Jackson said, helping himself to a seat on the futon.

"Where's Melody?" Frankie asked.

"Her parents are forcing her to have a family game night. She slept through the last one or something," Jackson said, pulling out his phone to send a quick text. "She says she'll try to come later. So, how does this work?" he asked, squinting against the glare of the bright white lights.

"Frankie will ask the questions from behind the camera, I'll shoot, and Heath will do audio," Brett explained, suddenly sounding very professional. "Make sure you look at her, not directly into the lens. Don't worry—your name won't be mentioned, and your face will be blurred."

"Ready?" Frankie asked, unfolding her list of ten interview questions.

Jackson pushed back the sleeves of his tan blazer and crossed his legs. The rubber toe of his black Converse was decorated with a giant *M* written in red ballpoint.

"Ready," he said.

"What makes you special?" Frankie began.

"You could say I have a split personality—there are two people living inside me."

"How did you end up this way?"

"My grandfather was Dr. Jekyll. He became addicted to a potion that gave him courage to act out his darkest fantasies. It altered his genetic code and was passed down to his son, my dad. Traces of it are in my blood. When I sweat, it comes out. The chemicals in my sweat trigger something in my brain. That trigger activates D.J. He's my other half."

"How long have you known about this?"

"About a week."

"When did you first notice that you were different?"

"I always knew I had blackouts, but I never knew I actually turned into a party guy named D.J. Hyde, until my girlfriend showed me a video of the transformation actually happening. I was blown away." Jackson began shaking his foot anxiously. Brett panned down to capture his stress.

"What is the best part about being a RAD?"

"Being part of a community that looks out for each other."

"What is the worst part about being a RAD?"

"Hiding."

"Do you consider yourself or D.J. dangerous?"

"Only to each other. My mom hasn't told him about me yet because she's not sure how he'll take the news. He might get jealous and try to keep me away or something. Also, I have a feeling D.J. doesn't study as much as I do. So he could do some serious damage to my GPA. And I'm not that into parties, so I might be a drain on his social life. But other than that kind of thing…no, not really."

"How would your life change if you didn't have to hide your identity?"

"I'd play sports 'cause I wouldn't have to worry about sweating. I'd hang out at the beach. My mom would be able to turn on the heat in the winter. Oh"—Jackson reached into the pocket of his blazer and pulled out his mini fan—"and I'd ditch this." He turned it on and held the plastic rotating blades to his face.

Frankie smiled and gave him a thumbs-up. The show-and-tell was great.

"Why did you agree to be in this film?"

"I want normies—uh—regular people to see that I'm a good person who is tired of hiding and tired of feeling ashamed of who I am."

"Thanks, Jackson, we're done."

"I thought you said there were ten questions," he said. "That was only nine."

Brett lowered his camera. "You have to ask him the last one. It will be the best part of the show."

"I think we're good," Frankie said, folding and refolding her questions until they could be folded no more. "We have six more interviews tonight. We have to stay on schedule."

"What was the question?" Jackson asked.

Frankie lowered her gaze.

"We were kinda hoping you would, you know, let us talk to D.J.," Brett said.

Jackson's ankle stopped jiggling. "You serious?"

Frankie wanted to jump through the felt-covered windows and bolt. Breaking up with D.J. would be hard enough. Did it really need to be done that night? In front of everyone?

"Dude, the transformation will be the hottest part of the show," Heath added.

"It *would* be cool," Brett said. "Normies would see that even at your worst, they have nothing to fear."

Frankie squirmed. She was uncomfortable with this, but Heath did have a point. It would be good for the show. And good for the show meant good for the RADs.

Jackson leaned back and considered this.

Frankie, Brett, and Heath waited silently.

"On one condition," Jackson finally said.

Frankie clenched her fists. She knew what was coming next.

"Break up with D.J."

"Break up?" Brett asked, shocked. "What are you talking about?"

"Please," Frankie rolled her eyes. "I didn't have my head on straight back then. It was a total rebound thing."

"Well, then I agree with Jackson," Brett said. "You should definitely break up with him."

"Why?" Frankie giggled.

Brett's pale cheeks burned red. She had her answer.

"Fine," she agreed. "Crank up the lights."

The shed was thick with heat. Frankie and the boys watched Jackson like a pot, but he refused to boil.

"Try jumping jacks," Brett suggested. The camera sat on a tripod, facing Jackson and ready for action. Brett was leaning against the wall, his cheeks flushed and his hair damp with sweat. Jackson jumped. The shed shook. Brett made him stop.

"What about push-ups?" Frankie suggested.

Jackson obediently got down on the ground and pushed himself up.

"How are you dry?" Heath asked, leaning against the blacked-out window and fanning his face with a bus schedule. "I can hardly breathe." He fanned harder, kicking up the dust from the window ledge. His eyelids fluttered, his nostrils twitched, and... ah...ah...ah-choo! He sneezed with gale force, unleashing a stream of fire. Before it could do any damage, it retracted back inside his mouth like slurped spaghetti.

Nobody moved. Peach-colored drops dripped from Frankie's fingertips like melted candle wax. Her Fierce & Flawless had liquefied.

Brett lifted his eye away from the camera's viewfinder and turned to his friend. "What the..." he whispered.

"I dunno," Heath shrugged. "It just started happening around my fifteenth birthday. Mostly when I burp or, you know—" He gestured to his butt. "Never when I sneeze. And the flames aren't usually this big."

"How come you never told me?" Brett asked, slightly offended.

"Dude, it's embarrassing."

They paused and looked at each other. The corners of their mouths curled up slowly as reality soaked its way into their brains.

"You're a RAD!" Brett shouted with joy.

"I'm a RAD!" Heath shouted back, his red eyebrows lifted in disbelief.

"Look," Frankie pointed at the futon.

Jackson, sweat-soaked and stunned, looked straight ahead while his eyes shifted from hazel to black, black to hazel, hazel to black, and finally to blue. His brown layers lightened two shades to a sandy blond, and a light dusting of stubble formed around his jawline.

That's new, thought Frankie.

D.J. had arrived.

"Smells like burned toast in here," he said, parting his hair from right to left. He took off Jackson's tan blazer, balled it up, and tossed it across the shed. "Firecracker!" He stood. "Where have you been?"

Stunned by the new physical transformation, Frankie spluttered to answer. "Uh, where have *you* been?" she countered.

D.J. scratched the back of his head. "Someone's a little needy." He smirked. "We just saw each other last night. Before I blacked out..."

"Actually, it was almost a week ago."

"It's okay. You don't have to make up stories. I think it's cute that you missed me. I missed you too." He paused. "Wait, what's Bekka's boyfriend doing here? What's with the camera?"

"We're making a movie about special people, and you're special, so we wanted to ask you some questions."

"As long as I get to ask you one when we're done," he said, rolling up the sleeves of Jackson's navy button-down and settling into the futon. Unlike his other half, D.J. splayed his arms over the back of the couch, a rock star between two invisible supermodels.

"Okay," Frankie agreed, hands shaking. "Here we go." She fumbled nervously through her notes, smearing makeup on the edge of the paper. "So, um, what makes you special?"

"I'm fun, I'm laid-back, and I get good grades without studying."

"How did you end up this way?"

"One part genes, two parts charm."

"Genes? Whose genes?" she pressed.

"Old man Hyde's. The man was a mad partier. I read his journals and, believe me, he was out there."

Frankie considered telling D.J. about Jackson right then and there. Imagine the footage! Oprah would have done it. But it wasn't Frankie's place. It was his mother's. *Their* mother's. All Frankie could do was skip a few questions and pray D.J. didn't see Jackson's interview when it aired.

"Why did you agree to be in this film?"

"Because you agreed to let me ask you a question."

Frankie giggled. He *was* charming. "Okay, what's your question?" She gestured for Brett to turn off his camera. He did immediately. She steeled herself for the inevitable, reminding her guilty conscience that hurting him would help Jackson, Melody,

Brett, and *her*. The benefits outweighed the costs in a mega way. Besides, he wasn't around that much anyway, so...

"I was wondering," D.J. asked, taking off Jackson's glasses. His blue eyes were brimming with sincerity. Suddenly, it didn't matter how well Frankie rationalized breaking his heart. She couldn't bring herself to do it. He didn't deserve it.

"Firecracker?"

"Yes," Frankie said to the rounded toe of her gray boots. Her bolts were starting to itch.

"Do you mind if we see other people?"

"*What?*" Frankie burst out laughing.

"I know you weren't expecting this," he said, reaching for her hand. "I'm sorry. It's just that my life is kind of all over the place right now, and I never know where I'm going to be from one minute to the next. And that's not fair to you."

Brett and Heath snickered.

"I totally understand." Frankie smiled. She opened the barn door, desperate for a rush of cool air and the return of Jackson.

But before the transformation occurred, she lifted her finger and gave D.J. a spark right on the cheek.

He rubbed the tiny red spot happily. "What was that for?"

"Something to remember me by."

"I'll always remember you, Firecracker." He winked.

Frankie's heart space swelled. Tiny electric happy faces rained down inside her like fireworks. And then his eyes turned black. Then blue. Then back to hazel.

Change was definitely in the air.

CHAPTER TWENTY
STALL WARS

Melody shoulder-leaned on the bathroom door, grateful that she had three minutes to pee before language arts class. One more class until the weekend—not that it really mattered. There would be no time for sleeping in. No time for a "halfway decent latte search" with Candace or a rom-com rental with Jackson. Not when she had to screen every single RAD interview they'd shot over the last eight days. Not when Ross was expecting a rough cut on Monday so he could give notes. Not when it aired on Thursday. NUDI duty called.

Instead of the typical third-floor bathroom smells, the scent of amber greeted Melody as she entered the girls' room. Beverly Hills Smellody would have darted for the second floor. But Salem Melody refused to run.

Cleo exited the middle stall and clomped toward the sink in her platform wood sandals. Gold triangles swung from her ears in perfect time with the flounce of the hem on her black and emerald-green mini. Her figure-skater style—emphasis on *figure*—was so uniquely her own, so incredibly flattering, that Melody couldn't help rethinking her boxy white tee, drawstring kakis, and navy mesh low-tops. She suddenly felt powerless, like a peasant in the presence of royalty.

"Hey," Melody said over the loud hum of the hand dryer. "Cute dress."

Cleo pressed the silver button for another blast of air.

She clearly blamed Melody for the botched *Teen Vogue* shoot, for the falling-out with her friends, and simply for having been born a normie. But it was easier to attract queen bees with honey than with vinegar, so Melody forced herself to be sweet.

"You know, I totally knew you were in here, 'cause I smelled your amber perfume, which is cool. I read that girls with a signature scent are more ambitious than girls without signature scents."

Cleo responded with a third blast of air.

Stay sweet…stay sweet…stay sweet…

"At lunch today, your friends were saying how much they missed you," Melody lied, ignoring the mounting pressure in her bladder. The truth was, Clawdeen had seen Cleo walking to class with Bekka and Haylee and had pretty much written her off for good. "They want you to come back."

Cleo finally made eye contact. "Oh, so you're sitting with them now too?" she snapped, fixing Melody with a paralyzing gaze.

Obviously, Cleo felt threatened. If ever there was a time for some peacekeeping sweetness, it was now. But all Melody could taste was vinegar.

"What's your problem?" she practically spat. "I'm just trying to help, and you act like I'm the Roman Empire or something."

Cleo's eyes widened to a warning. But Melody couldn't stop.

Assertiveness—combined with her ability to work in a historical metaphor—gave her more confidence than a figure-skater outfit ever could. "I'm not trying to dethrone you," Melody continued. "I'm just—"

"Shhh," Cleo hissed, gesturing toward the first stall, where a pair of peach UGG boots dangled above the vinyl flooring.

"Look," Melody whispered, refusing to let up, "I never meant to come between anyone. I'm just standing up for what I believe in."

"So am I," Cleo insisted, her triangle earrings swaying in concurrence.

"How? By choosing a fashion shoot? Is that all that matters to you? What about equal rights and—"

Cleo stomped her foot. "What are you talking about? Have you seriously lost your mind? Did the zombies get you too?"

"*What?*"

Melody searched Cleo's blue eyes for an explanation—a wink, a tear, a sign—a clue floating her way before she drowned in confusion. But Cleo offered nothing. Her gaze was hard and cold, just as Bekka's had been when she discovered the video of Jackson.

"Wait." Melody smirked. "I know what's happening. You've been hanging around with Bekka and—"

Bwoop. Bwoop. Last period was about to start. Still, Melody couldn't stop. Cleo was a queen bee-otch, but she deserved to know the truth.

"Bekka can't be trusted. You need to be careful."

The toilet flushed.

Bekka emerged.

Melody hurried into the last stall and slammed the door. But

189

embarrassment, anger, and regret found her anyway. How could she have been so dense? The peach UGGs, the sudden zombie comment, the wide eyes of warning? Cleo had tried to tell her, but Melody had been too seduced by her own voice to see the clues.

"Hey, Melodork," Cleo called over the running faucet. "Thanks for the warning."

Bekka burst out laughing, and then they were gone, leaving Melody behind to drown.

CHAPTER TWENTY-ONE
IT'S A WRAP

Merston High was dimly lit and empty. Anyone with a life renounced school on Sundays. But the kids without lives were the ones Cleo worried about; the ones who geeked out in the AV room until the weekend janitor sent them home. Because they would know that Cleo's visit to their tech temple was disingenuous. Not only would her exotic beauty stand out among their plainness like a calla lily in a cabbage patch, but she had never even considered entering their subterranean lair before — especially during prime tanning hours. If they didn't suspect white-collar crime, they'd assume Cleo couldn't afford her own computer. Neither theory would be good for her reputation.

So there she was, spending Sunday in the basement bathroom instead of with the three S's (sunning, shopping, spa-ing). Cleo was waiting for an "all clear" text from Bekka. As soon as the geeks were gone, Bekka would hack into Brett's computer and erase "The Ghoul Next Door." Which, thanks to Cleo's access to her friends' Facebook pages, they had learned Ross was expecting by the end of day on Monday. Cleo exhaled two weeks' worth of social angst into the chlorine-scented air. Finally, the end was near.

She checked her iPhone. Zero messages.

Ptah!

It was hard to believe that Deuce hadn't come around. He'd texted Cleo once, the night of their fight, asking her to "reconsider." She'd texted back THE MOVIE OR ME. To which he'd responded, BOTH. She typed WRONG ANSWER and cried into a heap of cat fur for hours.

It took all of her strength to play hard to get and not to pressure him to change his mind, especially since her heart-shaped hump was running dangerously low on reassurance. But if she didn't teach him the importance of putting his girlfriend above everything else, who would?

But her friends? She definitely thought they would have come back by now. Which is why she hadn't told *Teen Vogue* they were short two models and one stylist's assistant. With the shoot only four days away, her need to fess up was becoming more urgent. Cleo's professional connections were at stake, not to mention her father's trust. If she told the truth now, the magazine could find replacements. But the day of? Would they even want to?

Cleo checked her phone again. Still no messages. Were her friends really having fun without her? Was it even possible?

Still, Cleo clung to hope.

Ping!

If it weren't for Bekka's constant HUNT updates, Cleo's cell phone would die from loneliness.

A pink rubber-gloved hand reached out and yanked Cleo into the computer-packed room. "Hurry," Haylee insisted, shutting the door behind them and securing the window shade. Her stakeout ensemble—a peach boyfriend cardi over mauve-and-gray-striped leggings—couldn't have been more conspicuous if it flashed neon and blasted death metal.

"Hey," Bekka called from the third row of computers. She was already clacking away but paused to wave her blue rubber-gloved hand. "This is easier than I thought. I should be done in a minute."

Cleo winced, fanning the musty air. It smelled like flying coach beside a passenger eating nacho cheese Doritos. Cans of soda and balled-up fast-food wrappers overflowed the trash can by the door, as if trying to escape the maddening hum of machines and unflattering fluorescent lights.

"Here," Haylee said, reaching into her attaché case and pulling out a pair of red wool mittens. "Put these on before you touch anything."

Cleo pinched the itchy mitts as if they were covered in poo.

"Oh, and here's a HUNT wristband," she said, sliding a mangled yellow bracelet off her wrist. "I melted down my old LIVE-STRONG bracelets, and voilà!"

"Seriously?"

Haylee lowered her tortoiseshell frames and glared at Cleo in a *why-wouldn't-I-be-serious?* sort of way.

"It looks like chewed gum."

"Perfect." Haylee snickered. "Since we're trying to *stick* together."

Good Geb! Are all normies this scary? Cleo wanted to tell Haylee where to *stick* her itchy mitts and clumpy bracelet, but she wasn't going to get into a power struggle now. Why ruin an already ruined Sunday? Besides, HUNT was only a means to an end. And that end was near.

"What can I do?" Cleo asked, trying not to inhale.

"HIDE!" Haylee whisper-shouted.

"What?" Cleo turned.

"Get down and turn off your ringers!"

Haylee sprinted from her post and tackled Cleo to the ground. Together they crawled across the crumb-covered carpet to the end of the third row. Knees burning, Cleo regretted her decision to wear a miniskirt almost as much as she regretted having joined this ragtag operation. Knowing Haylee, this was probably just a drill.

They scurried under the long rectangular table and joined up with Bekka.

"Who was it?" Cleo whispered, rearranging her black-and-pink chiffon banded mini to prevent a Cosabella sighting.

"Brett!" mouthed Haylee. "And—"

The door squeaked open. A pair of scuffed hiking boots and knee-high platform boots entered.

Frankie!

The feet hurried inside, and the couple sat by a computer in the first row.

What are they doing here? Cleo asked with raised brows.

Bekka responded with a shrug of her shoulders. *You tell me. Isn't that your job?* her bugged-out eyes asked.

We're dead, Haylee said by finger-slicing her neck.

Cleo lifted her gaze in reverence to Hathor. She was about to ask for guidance and protection, but when she saw a constellation of crusty boogers and mashed Skittles on the underside of the table, she decided not to involve the goddess in this one.

"Ready?" Frankie asked.

Someone began typing, then stopped after a few seconds and sighed.

"Ready," said Brett.

"Good luck."

"I couldn't have done it without you. I mean, I *wouldn't* have done it without you," he said. Then came the sound of kissing.

Bekka rolled her green eyes, which were starting to tear. She lowered her head and hid, softly sniffling, behind the sway of her wavy bob.

Cleo was starting to feel sorry for her. Watching Melody revenge-kiss Deuce had made her sweat amber for an entire weekend—and Deuce had been *attacked*. She couldn't imagine how Bekka felt knowing that Brett actually *liked* Frankie. And Cleo wasn't going to try. She couldn't! Bekka was the enemy. She was dangerous. No matter how pathetic she might look at the moment.

Boop...

Someone began dialing on speakerphone.

Boop...boop. Boop...boop...boop...boop.

"Ross Healy," answered a man after the first ring.

"Whaddup? It's Brett."

"And Frankie." She giggled.

Bekka rolled her eyes.

"We just sent it," Brett said.

Cleo gasped, then covered her mouth. *Just sent it? Today? But it's not due until tomorrow!*

Bekka shot her a *how-could-you-screw-this-up?* glare. Cleo flicked some carpet fluff off the side of her shoe, pretending not to notice.

"Hey, B-man, thanks again for getting it in a day early. The network is dying to see it."

"As long as they know it's rough," Brett reminded him. "But I can change whatever. So just let me know."

"You got it. Thanks again, B-doggy-dog. I'll be in touch."

The line went dead.

"I hope this works," Brett said, sounding nervous.

"It will," Frankie assured him. "You'll see."

If only someone were there to reassure Cleo. Someone to tell her she hadn't just blown the biggest opportunity of her life. Someone to tell her she'd find a way to get her friends back. Someone to tell her this movie wouldn't change life as she knew it, even though it already had. Because that life was good. Things went her way. People listened to her. And no one—

A cell phone rang.

"Hey," Brett answered on speaker. "Everything okay?"

"Everything's great, *Brett*," said Ross. "As long as you tell me this is a joke and you're sending me the real movie in zero-point-two seconds."

196

Bekka lifted her head.

There is a Geb!

"Whaddaya mean?" Brett asked.

"What do I mean? I mean, what's with all the blurred faces?" Ross shouted. "Our viewers are going to think they have cataracts. We can't air this. Send me the clean cut."

Bekka and Haylee exchanged a luminous smile and a silent high five. This is exactly what they wanted—*proof*! And exactly what the RADs feared.

Another botched job by Frankie Stein. What a shock!

Now what? worried Cleo. A clean cut would be the end of the RADs. Their identities would be exposed. Their images would be downloaded all over the world. They would become targets. Medical experiments. Scapegoats. No matter how docile and charming the interviews were, normies would find some reason to be afraid. Some reason to discriminate. Some reason to hate. They always did.

Cleo wanted to sink into a lavender-scented bath. She wanted to snuggle with her cats and laugh with her friends. She wanted a Sunday full of the three S's and text messages and Deuce. But that life seemed like centuries ago.

"So, are you sending it?" Ross asked.

"Uh," Brett groaned.

Stop him, Frankie!

"Brett?"

Frankie! Stop him. Don't let him do it!

"Are we cool?"

"*We* are," Frankie said. "But *you're* not!"

Cleo bit her bottom lip. Not bad for a bolt head.

"B-man?" Ross asked, dismissing Frankie.

"Sorry. I can't."

"You're kidding, right? This is a huge opportunity," Ross pressed.

"I know." Brett sighed. "But I promised."

"Promised who?"

"My friends," Brett countered.

Ross chuckled. "These freaks are your *friends*?"

"Yes, and they need to be protected."

"He has integrity, you know," Frankie added.

"Do you really think you're going to make it in this business with *integrity*?"

"No," Brett said. "I'll make it with my talent."

"Come on, kid. Talent has nothing to do with success."

"Yeah, R-man." Brett chuckled. "I knew that the minute I met *you*."

The line went dead.

Frankie and Brett were silent. It was over.

Golden!

Cleo tried to mirror the frustration on Bekka's and Haylee's faces but stopped for fear of looking constipated. All she wanted to do was bust out from under the table and leave berry-scented lip prints on every computer screen in the room. Geb had saved her once again. "The Ghoul Next Door" was ancient history! She didn't have to betray anyone! No crime. No time. She pulled off the red mitts and let them fall to the carpet. She was free!

"I'm so sorry," Frankie said. "You worked so hard on this."

"It's okay," Brett said kindly.

"No, it's not." Frankie sniffled. "I shorted it again!"

"How? You promised to keep everyone safe, and you did."

There was a short pause and then another sniffle. "They're going to be so disappointed. How are we going to tell them?"

"Together."

Awww. Liquid warmth filled Cleo like the melted chocolate inside Hasina's molten lava cake. Brett was pretty decent for a normie.

The door to the lab closed with a defeated click.

Cleo emerged from under the table and smoothed her skirt. Either the fluorescent lights were making her hands look ashen or stress had faded her in a big way. "You think it's still sunny outside?"

Bekka shrugged, wiped her cheeks dry, and stood.

"Now what?" Haylee asked the HUNT leader as she scooted out from under the table.

"We start over."

"I couldn't agree more." Cleo hooked her ruffled denim tote over her shoulder. "See ya on the other side." Without another word, she crossed the grimy carpet and walked out. Each step that echoed in the empty hall brought her closer to starting over—and proving that there was, indeed, a life after death.

TO: RADs
Oct 10, 5:13 PM
FRANKIE: IF U R INVOLVED IN THE MOVIE, THERE'S A 911 MEETING IN MY BACKYARD 2MORROW AFTER SCHOOL @ 3:30 PM. NO BLANKETS REQUIRED. IT WILL BE SHORT. XXXXX

CHAPTER TWENTY-TWO
MUMMY'S HOME

Cleo was the first to arrive. As before, she followed the sound of rushing water through the leafy thicket and emerged in the Steins' secret backyard. The rock-bottomed falls were still flowing and frothing. The grassy perimeter was still manicured and damp. And mist still danced above the stone ledges of the pool. But this time the visit felt completely different. Because this time Cleo was freshly spray-tanned and thrilled to be there.

A late afternoon breeze blew her bangs skyward. It was much too chilly for her bronze minidress and black satin booties with the bows on the back, but Cleo was feeling too festive for anything less. "Hey," she chirped.

Frankie was sitting alone on the ledge, finger-batting her wrist seams like a cat with yarn. "Hey," she mumbled, her head still down. Even her gray terry sweats looked miserable.

"Laundry day?"

Frankie lifted her eyes. Normally periwinkle, their hue had been downgraded to plain blue against her SillyPutty-colored makeup.

"What happened? You're toting bigger bags than Mary-Kate Olsen!" Cleo remarked.

"Whatever."

Cleo considered recommending cold cucumber slices, a steaming mug of Hasina's skin-replenishing Nile elixir, and a more inspired comeback. After all, Frankie had proved herself to be a noble warrior by rejecting Ross, and she deserved some kindness. But *that* wouldn't kick in until Cleo was absolutely sure "The Ghoul Next Door" was "The Ghoul No More."

"What are you doing here, anyway?" Frankie asked, more shocked than bothered.

"I got your text about the movie." Cleo sat. "And if it's not too late, I want to be in it."

"Ha!" said Frankie with her mouth closed. After that, there was nothing more she was willing to share. At least not until the others arrived. So they waited together in silence.

Before long the yard was buzzing with RADs. They greeted one another warmly, with hugs and energetic high fives. No longer a passive group bound solely by secrets, they saw themselves as a force—a proactive faction on a do-or-die mission to change the world. And their pride was palpable. All around Cleo, bubbles of conversation rose and popped, sprinkling the yard with giddy enthusiasm.

"HBO is gonna be all over this. They love edgy dramas."

"Really? I see it more as a comedy."

"Or a Broadway musical."

"Oh, and you *know* some author will try to turn it into a teen series."

"You think Oprah would put it in her book club?"

"Of course. She's a sucker for outcasts."

"Funny, I thought *you* were the sucker."

"Funny, I thought *you* were funny."

"Have you seen Jackson's sketches? He drew doll versions of all of us."

"Imagine getting yourself in a Happy Meal?"

"Yum. I imagine it all the time. By the way, is it me or is someone grilling a tenderloin?"

Despite being ignored by her closest friends, Cleo felt surprisingly good. In fact, she felt regal. Like a stoic queen privy to the impending doom of her people, she accepted her solitude as a by-product of her wisdom, an *it's-lonely-at-the-top* sort of thing. But she wouldn't be lonely much longer. Frankie was calling the meeting to order, and in a matter of minutes, these conversation bubbles would burst. And the *Teen Vogue* shoot would be right there to sop up the mess.

"Thanks for coming," Frankie said.

The applause was uproarious. Amid the fervor, Lala, Blue, and Clawdeen kept casting sidelong glances at Cleo, probably wondering why she was there. Deuce winked at her but chose to remain with his fellow cast members. Julia stared at Frankie expectantly, in her usual zombielike state. Claude and the other Wolf brothers howled triumphantly. Melody and Jackson were at the very front of the crowd, wearing smiles so wide that the corners of their mouths nearly fused. They had no clue what was coming.

Frankie stepped up onto the stony ledge, just as she'd done before. But this time she made no attempt to silence the booming falls. Viveka and Viktor stood at the back of the crowd, eyes low. They already knew.

"I'll keep it short because most of us have a bio quiz tomorrow—"

"Yeah, thanks a lot, Jackson," Claude shouted gruffly from the back of the crowd.

"What does it have to do with *me*?" Jackson blushed.

"Ms. J is *your* mom."

"Well, she's *your* teacher. And she said she's gonna be your teacher again next year if you don't pass this quiz."

Everyone laughed at Jackson as if he were Chris Rock. It felt more like open-mike night at the Improv than a Monday after school.

"Hey!" Frankie sparked. Brett stood solemnly by her side. "Just stop talking for a second and listen, okay?"

The crowd quieted.

"We worked really hard on 'The Ghoul Next Door' and—"

Claude snickered.

"Dude!" Brett snapped. "This is serious. The movie isn't happening. Channel Two isn't going to air it."

Frankie pouted big enough for all of them. A chorus of shouts came from the RADs.

"What?"

"Fur real?"

"You're bloody joking, mate. Right?"

"Of course he's joking. Why wouldn't they air it?"

Cleo crossed her spray-tanned legs and closed her eyes. She felt as though she were sinking into that hot bath, but instead of water, justice washed over her. And instead of lavender, the bathwater was infused with the soothing aroma of *you-should-have-stuck-with-me.*

"The network people said they'd air the piece only if we showed your faces," Brett explained.

"They can't do that!"

"It would destroy us!"

"We refused," Frankie assured them.

The yard was silent except for the sound of crashing water. For a second, Cleo actually felt sorry for her friends. Not for their loss of fame but for their failed attempt at freedom.

"Right on, Frank-ay!" someone shouted. Billy started to clap.

The applause was scant at first but began to mount until everyone in the yard was cheering for Frankie and her NUDI crush. Their support lingered, but their giddy enthusiasm was gone. The light had drained from their eyes. Their fire had smoldered to a thin ribbon of smoke.

Cleo stood with grace. Rolling back her glistening shoulders, she crossed the lawn. Weaving unnoticed through the crowd of bodies, she felt like a ghost on a quest to reclaim her lost soul.

Clawdeen saw her first. Her yellow-brown eyes, like two tiger-eye stones, bore right into Cleo. Once the inspiration for Cleo's first jewelry collection, those eyes seemed hard and cold.

"Hey," Cleo managed to stammer.

Clawdeen nudged Lala and Blue. All three girls were glaring now.

"What are you doing here?" Lala asked.

Red lipstick was smudged on her chin, but Cleo didn't dare to comment. "I came to see if I could help with the movie, and then..."

"What about your precious modeling career?" Clawdeen barked.

"I canceled the shoot. You guys were right. This is more important."

The girls exchanged validated grins. Cleo was about to elaborate on the fake "tongue-lashing from Anna Wintour, who had high hopes for the budding designer-slash-model," when a distractingly warm breeze blew against her shoulder. It smelled like lemon Starburst. "Billy, stop spying!"

"Oh, sorry. I didn't know this conversation was private."

"If you don't get out of here, I'm going to spray you with self-tanner. And then you'll know exactly what private is." Cleo wiggled her baby finger. "We all will."

The girls couldn't help giggling.

"Later, hater," Billy groaned. The lemon-scented breeze was gone.

"So," Blue said, her blue eyes back to bizzo. "You reckon you'll be able to get the modeling shoot back? You know, now that the movie is bogged."

"I dunno. I haven't really thought about it." Cleo sighed. "I guess I could try."

Clawdeen twirled an auburn curl around her finger. Her long nails were painted with yellow and brown pinstripes. "You think they'd take us back too? Or did you already promise the job to your new best friends?"

Cleo knit her professionally arched brows in confusion.

"Bekka and Haylee," Lala offered.

"No way! I would never ask them to model. Have you seen their bone structure? It's so...normal."

The other girls nodded in agreement.

"So, there's a chance we can still do it?" Clawdeen asked.

"You know, if we practice our poses and do our squint-prevention exercises?"

"I guess," Cleo said casually. "If you really want to."

They nodded and squealed and told her they really, really, really, really did.

"Clawdeen, I was thinking," said Cleo, leaning over to touch her friend's curly hair. "You could wear the earrings on your birthday if you want—maybe for a glamorous Sweet Sixteen photo!"

"Really?" Clawdeen squealed. "That would be amazing!"

"Does this mean you forgive me for being so selfish?" Cleo asked.

"Do you forgive us for being so judgmental?" Lala countered.

"Only if you forgive me for telling you to wipe that lipstick off your chin."

"Thanks a lot," Lala snapped at Blue and Clawdeen. "Why didn't you tell me?"

"We were too busy looking at your wonky eyeliner to notice." Blue giggled.

They all busted out laughing. Deuce glanced over and gave Cleo a *way-to-get-your-friends-back* thumbs-up. Cleo winked back just as her friends pulled her into a group hug. She'd deal with Deuce later.

"*Mummy's home!*" Lala exclaimed.

"Mummy's home." Cleo smiled.

TO: Clawdeen, Lala, Blue
Oct 11, 9:28 PM
CLEO: SHOOT IS ON. YOU'RE IN! I'LL BE AT THE LOCATION
ALL DAY. MAGAZINE IS SENDING A LIMO 4 U. WILL PICK U
UP AFTER LAST PERIOD THURSDAY. ^^^^^^^

TO: Cleo
Oct 11, 9:29 PM
CLAWDEEN: GOOD THING I FORGOT TO CANCEL MY WAX
APPT! CAN'T WAIT!! THX. ####

TO: Cleo
Oct 11, 9:31 PM
LALA: FANG-TASTIC!!!!!! :::::::::::::::

TO: Cleo
Oct 11, 9:33 PM
BLUE: GOBSMACKED! @@@@@@

CHAPTER TWENTY-THREE
RAD RAGE

Bwoop. Bwoop.

Today, the bell was supposed to signify more than the last period of the day. It should have been a call to arms. A countdown to the millennial RADs' inaugural television address. An invitation to an after-party in Brett's shed to celebrate their first sanctioned outing since the 1930s. But it might as well have been "Taps"—the solemn bugle composition played at military funerals—that Frankie was hearing. Because her dreams were dead.

Normies would never know how hard Claude Wolf was working for a sports scholarship. They'd never see Deuce's impressive 381-piece sunglasses collection or hear about Blue's hope of becoming a pro surfer. They'd never cry with Clawdeen while she relived the terror of being sprayed red by PETA activists or having to shower in the locker room after gym class. Never identify with Jackson's embarrassing battle with sweat or sympathize with D.J.'s lack of control over his life. Lala's refusal to smile would continue to fuel her reputation as shy, and Julia's zombie stare would always be mistaken for stupidity. Heath would have to stay indoors during allergy season. Poor Billy would never be able to date a girl who didn't want to be accused of talking to herself. Frankie would remain hidden under the Spackle of pore-clogging makeup and yurtlike garments. And Brett and Melody would be burdened with keeping their RAD friends' secrets.

Even though their faces would have been blurred, and the movie would not have solved all their problems, it would have been a first step—one they were finally willing to take together. One that hadn't been taken in eighty years. One that had gone nowhere. Sure, Frankie could try again. But she was fresh out of ideas. Besides, who would trust her now? Everything she touched turned to mold.

It was obvious by the unusual silence that the others heard "Taps" too. Clawdeen, Blue, and Lala were the only RADs who didn't seem affected by the lost cause. How could they be, when they were about to be picked up by a shiny black limo with a window sign that said TEEN VOGUE? Holding hands, they ran through the halls with the subtlety of an old clunker trailing cans and a JUST MARRIED sign down an asphalt road. But instead of scratch marks on pavement, they left behind a sickly sweet trail of fruity lotion, floral perfume, and friends moving on.

Suddenly, Melody appeared at Frankie's locker, panting. "You're not going to believe it!" Her cheeks were flushed, her gray eyes wide, her black hair a wild mess. Her beauty was undeniable, and she didn't have to wear a stitch of makeup. A pinch of envy kept Frankie from asking what was wrong. After all, how bad could it be? Melody's life was perfect.

"Candace is home sick," Melody continued.

"Bummer," Frankie said, sensing the hollowness in her own voice. "I hope she feels better soon." She closed her locker and hooked her silver-studded backpack over her shoulder.

"Please, she's totally faking," Melody went on. "But she was watching TV and saw a promo for 'The Ghoul Next Door.' Channel Two is airing it!"

Frankie began walking toward the exit. Melody ran alongside her like a puppy.

"It must be a mistake," Frankie decided, refusing to hope. "I'm sure someone would have called us."

"It's not a mistake. Candace called the station. They're airing it!"

"Are you sure?"

Melody nodded.

VOLTAGE!

Frankie stopped in the middle of the hall, ignoring the accidental elbow bumps from passing students, and texted Brett the news.

He appeared beside them within seconds. "Are you sure?" he asked.

Melody told him about Candace's news.

"Why wouldn't Ross call me?"

The girls shrugged.

"What made him change his mind about blurring everyone's face?"

"Maybe he felt guilty," Melody suggested.

"But I thought they wanted to show everyone watching the broadcast in the studio."

"Just call him," Frankie urged.

Brett tried Ross four times, his black-polished fingers dialing the number with uncontainable pep. But each time his call went straight to voice mail. "Oh, well," he said, too excited to get discouraged. "Let's have a screening party. Can you guys get everyone to the shed by five thirty? I'll set up and order some pizza."

They parted ways with renewed purpose. Frankie lifted her matronly, floor-dusting peasant skirt as she hurried down the school steps to spread the shocking good news.

In a little over an hour, Brett had transformed his monster museum into a cushy screening room. He'd hung a flat-screen TV, created four rows of mismatched seating, and set up a table stacked with pizza boxes, sodas, and bowls of candy. He left the doors open to keep Jackson from overheating. He had a fire extinguisher standing by for Heath, marked three of the Domino's boxes MEAT LOVER'S for the Wolfs, and even had a space heater on hand in case Lala stopped by after the photo shoot. The vase of green tulips was for Frankie.

The room quickly filled with people buzzing about the twist of fate. And at least five of them told Frankie how lucky she was to be with Brett. Not Brett the normie. Not Brett the NUDI. Not Brett, Bekka's ex. The qualifiers were gone. The lines had been blurred. He was no longer separate from them. He was just Brett. It was a good sign. If this group could come around, anyone could.

"Here we go," he called, cranking up the volume.

The chewing and the chatter stopped. Everyone settled into

chairs with squirmy anticipation. Brett stood by the screen, unable to contain his excitement. It reminded Frankie of herself only two weeks ago, standing with her nose practically pressed against the TV while she watched him in the hospital. The unpredictability of life made her smile. One minute her head was coming off, and the next her heart was on her sleeve. Frankie Stein was finally living!

Everyone cheered when Ross appeared on the screen. He was standing in front of the Merston High letter board. His boyish features were the perfect complement to a story about judgments based on looks. With his smooth skin, wide brown eyes, and dimple-studded smile, he seemed more likely to scoop ice cream than the news.

"Should he be showing our school?" asked Deuce.

No one answered. They were waiting breathlessly to see where this was going. Julia nervously pushed her glasses up her nose.

"It's Spotlight on Oregon week here on Channel Two, and our slogan, "It's all true on Two," has never been more, well, *true*." He snickered. "Two weeks ago, I received a red-hot tip that there were monsters—yes, *monsters*—living right here in Salem." He strolled around to the other side of the board. There, the letters had been rearranged to say MONSTER HIGH. "It's everyone's worst nightmare come true...or is it?"

"Did he just say 'nightmare'?" asked Claude, gnashing his teeth.

"Shhh," everyone hissed.

"What you're about to see are interviews I was able to gather from these monsters. Some will have you laughing. Some will have you crying. But all of them will tell you everything you need to know about 'The Ghoul Next Door.'"

The show's title, which bled red, spun onto the screen and throbbed to the theme music from the movie *Psycho*.

"What happened to my graphics?" Jackson called.

Puuuurp.

"Sorry," Heath said as a band of fire shot out the back of his chair. "That sausage pizza was super spicy."

Suddenly, the shed felt more like a sauna. But no one seemed to notice—because Bekka had appeared on the screen. Wearing a frilly white dress and too much blush, she was seated in what looked like a church pew. Everyone gasped.

"What's she doing there?" Brett asked the TV.

Melody leaned over and whispered, "What's happening?"

Frankie tugged her neck seams. "I have no idea."

The camera pushed in tight on Bekka's freckly face as she began to speak. "Hi. I'm Bekka Madden. My boyfriend, Brett, made the following film, but it was made under duress. The creatures you are about to see have possessed him. They have turned him into their propaganda zombie, forcing him to shoot these scenes to gain your trust. Once they have it, they'll steal your souls and suck your minds. But this is not a time for panic. It's a time for action. Stop them before they stop you. And, Brett, if you're watching, I love you. You can come back now. I'll keep you safe."

How did this happen? Why did it happen? Who let it happen?

The show began immediately with an *unblurred* interview with Jackson.

Melody gasped.

"Brett, what are they doing?" Jackson shouted.

"I have no idea!"

214

"We were tricked!" Claude howled, whipping a slice of meat lover's pizza at the TV screen. It stuck and slid, landing with a *thonk* on the floor.

"Everyone will know where we live!"

"We'll never be allowed back in school!"

"What about my scholarship?"

"Where are we going to hide now?"

"How will we even get there?"

"My parents are going to kill me."

"I'm already dead, and mine are *still* going to kill me."

"I'll never get to play Juliet now."

"I was supposed to take my road test tomorrow!"

"There's a geek living inside of me!" D.J. shouted, his face covered in sweat. "Why didn't my mother tell me? Why didn't any of *you* tell me?" He pushed through the cramped rows of chairs and ran out of the shed.

"D.J., wait!" Deuce called. But it was too late. He was gone.

"My bad," Heath said, blushing.

"D.J. is right. We should get outta here!"

"Omigod, how do we stop this?" Melody asked amid the growing chaos.

"I have no idea," Frankie said, trembling.

Her cell rang. She answered on speaker, to avoid shorting the phone with her spraying bolts.

"Is this fur *real*?" Clawdeen barked.

Frankie opened her mouth, but no sound came out.

"Cleo must have known about this," Clawdeen continued. "She's been BFFs with Bekka for the last two weeks. She had to be involved."

"Why would she do this to us?" Lala shouted in the background.

"What are you so worried about?" Blue cried. "At least no one can see *your* face."

Frankie's insides churned. "Are you at the shoot?" she asked, not knowing what else to say.

"In the limo. We were on our way to the shoot, but we saw the whole thing on the TV in the car. I don't want to see Cleo or another camera for the rest of my life! We're turning around and coming home. That is, if our driver doesn't kill us first. He keeps checking his rearview mirror and asking why he can't see Lala. He thinks we're playing monster mind tricks on him. I swear he's driving at least a hundred and forty right now. We were crazy to trust Cleo. I hope a camel takes a steaming hot...*SLOW DOWN!*" she shouted. "We're not going to hurt you, okay? Frankie, you should watch out for Brett and Melody. They probably masterminded this whole thing with Bekka."

Melody gasped. "That is so not true!" she shouted into the speaker.

"Oh, really? Because we were doing fine until you showed up."

"Clawdeen, I would never—"

"Don't listen to her, Frankie. Just get out of there as fast as you can. We'll be home soon. Unless this maniac kills us. I said *SLOW DOWN!*"

The line went dead.

Frankie didn't know where to turn. Was Clawdeen onto something? Her theory *did* made sense. Brett and Bekka...dating forever. He's a budding filmmaker looking for a break...and he stumbles on the story of the century. They mastermind a plan...

send Brett and Melody to work from the inside...to build her trust and win her heart. His shed was a set piece...the posters of Grandpa Stein were props...a complex scheme with a single goal in mind...to go viral...global...Hollywood.

"How could you do this to us?" Frankie shouted at Melody.

"Seriously, Frankie, I have no idea what you're talking about."

Her weak response didn't deserve another minute of Frankie's attention. Melody was nothing more than a pretty face that had been used (like the rest of them) to further Brett and Bekka's quest for immortality. Ironically, immortality was something so many RADs came by naturally. But Brett and Bekka had to go for it the normie way — by selling their souls for fame.

"You lied to me!" Frankie shouted. But her words got lost in the barrage of insults, threats, and finger foods being hurled at Brett. Still, she kept right on screaming. Brett just stood by the TV, motionless, silently accepting his flogging.

"Run!" Deuce called. "He won't stay stoned forever."

En masse, the RADs bolted from the shed and fanned out into the street in a complete free-for-all. All sense of unity was gone. They were running for their lives once again. Frankie didn't know whether to chase after them, topple Brett to the ground, or call her parents and urge them to start packing.

So she ran.

She ran and ran and ran with no destination in mind. Sparking and sobbing her way down Baker Street, Frankie couldn't help thinking that maybe Cleo had been right. Maybe Viktor should take her apart.

Because if he didn't, someone else would.

CHAPTER TWENTY-FOUR
SIREN SAYS

"D.J.?" Melody called as she turned onto Piper Lane. "Jack-sonnn?"

No one answered. So she kept running and calling. Tree-lined street after tree-lined street, she called and ran, avoiding cars and interrupting games of street soccer.

"D.J.? Jackson?" she called on Dewey Crescent.

"D.J.? Jackson?" she called on Willow Way.

"D.J.? Jackson?" she called on Narrow Pine Road.

Still no one answered.

Thirty minutes after the mass exodus from the shed, she was still running and calling. And never once did she have to stop for a blast from her inhaler. In fact, she could have kept going if she'd thought it would do any good. That was the silver lining on this horribly cloudy evening.

It sickened her to the point of nausea when she thought about Brett and Bekka's ploy. How much it had set the RADs back—

not to mention her place among them—and for what? Bekka's pride? Brett's career? A rush?

Melody slowed to a walk. All this running wasn't getting her anywhere. The bigger question was, *What now?* Keep searching for D.J. and Jackson? Convince Frankie she had nothing to do with the TV show? Hide the RADs in her house? Have her father carve them into normies? Find Bekka and Brett, slather them in steak sauce, and leave them on the Wolfs' doorstep? Yes, yes, yes, yes, and *yes!*

Or she could confront the one person no one wanted to talk to. The one who probably had the answers. The one who needed Melody as much as much as Melody needed her, whether she knew it yet or not.

Sitting on a curb, she dialed Candace. The red *J* Jackson had written on the rubber toe of her black Converse had smudged and started to fade. *Is it a sign? Does he need me? Am I making the right choice? What if*—

"Ah-choo!" *Sniff.* "Hullo? Mel?" Candace answered. "Obighod, did you see that show? Dis can't be good, right? Ah-choo!"

Melody rolled her eyes. "I know you're faking, Can. You can talk normally."

"Fine, what do you want?"

"You have to report for NUDI duty. I need a ride."

Melody bit her lip, dreading the shrill sound of Candace's *you-gotta-be-kidding-me* laugh.

"Where? When? Wardrobe?"

"Really?" Melody asked, shocked that Candace had agreed so easily. "Um, corner of Forest and Cliff. Now. Formfitting. Oh, and bring something for me too. I'm kinda sweaty. Hurry!"

"Candace out!"

While Melody waited, she dialed Jackson's number, but her call went straight to his voice mail each time. The same thing happened when she tried to reach Frankie. Melody got up, stretched her legs as she leaned against the side of a tree, and called again. And again. And again. *What if their phones have been confiscated? What if they're in the back of a paddy wagon heading for Alcatraz? What if…*

Weeeoooo weeeoooo weeoooooo.

The sound of an approaching police siren froze Melody's thoughts to fear-cicles. The roundup had begun.

Weeeoooo weeeoooo weeoooooo.

She stood.

Weeeoooo weeeoooo weeoooooo.

Her stomach was now in her throat. Her arms were shaking with fright; her legs were twitching with flight.

Weeeoooo weeeoooo weeoooooo.

A forest-green BMW SUV screeched as it rounded the corner onto Cliff. The sirens got louder, but the paddy wagon was nowhere in sight.

"Hey!" Candace shouted over the siren blaring in her car. Thin braids appeared randomly throughout her mess of blond curls. She wore a strapless yellow silk-chiffon minidress, a peacock-feather necklace, and strappy turquoise booties. Her body had been dusted in shimmering bronze powder and spritzed with enough Black Orchid perfume to blow a second hole in the ozone layer. "Hop in!"

"What is *that*?" Melody shouted back, covering her ears.

"A police car sound effect. I downloaded it. As the NUDI

driver, I thought I might need it someday. Don't worry about the ninety-nine cents. It's a tax write-off."

"Well, can you turn it down?" Melody asked, hopping into the passenger seat. "I have enough noise in my head right now."

"Fine." Candace shrugged. "Siren out."

And off they went.

CHAPTER TWENTY-FIVE
SAVED BY THE MEL

Seated on a foldout throne made of black canvas and wood, Cleo gazed out of the white holding tent, feeling every part the Egyptian queen. Frantic worker bees buzzed all around her, running wires, cleaning camera lenses, and attempting to roll wardrobe racks through the sand.

Like the regal women who had come before her, she gazed out at the golden dunes, marveling at the amber-scented breeze and how it shaped and shifted the terrain with the delicate strokes of an artist's brush. It was as if Ra had commissioned the wind to create beauty just for her.

In the old days, moments like this would have been preserved on dusty walls, portrayed by crude drawings of vultures, disembodied legs, and zigzags. Thankfully, times had changed. As soon as her friends arrived, Cleo would be photographed by Kolin VanVerbeentengarden, lit by Tumas, and featured in *Teen Vogue*. If only the magazine could find its way to the afterlife. Aunt Nefertiti would be blown away.

After three hours of wardrobe and jewelry fittings, two hours of hair and makeup, a luxurious Dead Sea salt foot scrub, and a mani-pedi, Cleo was ready for her close-up. She was also ready for her medium shot, her sultry shot, her action shot, her regal shot, her *I'm-too-sexy-for-this-camel* shot, and her shot at making a name for herself in the highly competitive world of jewelry design. Her sketches and samples were locked away in the safe of Manu's Bentley, patiently waiting for their turn in the spotlight. And they would get it, as soon as she had impressed the editors with her professionalism and her well-rehearsed repertoire of poses.

An emaciated intern pulled up to the holding tent in an ATV. "Any word yet?" she asked. Her hair was tied back with a Pucci scarf and reinforced with a pair of white-framed Guccis. A sheer lime-green tank billowed over her pore-clogging skinny jeans.

Um, who is the model here?

"Jaydra doesn't want to wait any longer. We're losing light."

Where are they?

Cleo lowered her head and checked her phone again. She had service and plenty of battery left. But no new text messages. The beads on her gold headdress clinked together for what was bound to be the last time if Clawdeen, Blue, and Lala didn't show up.

"They should have been here two hours ago. I don't understand," she managed to croak, despite what felt like a giant hairball stuck in her throat. "What if there was an accident?"

"Then you have three minutes to scrape them off the roadway, or this shoot is canceled," the intern snapped, slamming her YSL cork wedge on the gas and rumbling off.

Cleo could send another message, but what was the point? She had already sent eleven, in varying tones, and had yet to get a single response. Normally Cleo might have wondered if her friends were mad. But not today. They had texted all through last period, counting down the seconds until they could join her on the set.

Cleo checked the Saran that had been wrapped around her feet to preserve her pedi. Then she heel-waddled toward her bald savior.

"Manu," she whined, choking back tears that would land her right back in the makeup trailer. "Have you found them *yet*?"

He stood at the back of the tent with four officers who had been charged with guarding the jewels. Manu checked three cell phones at once. He lifted his dark eyes and grinned. "They are pulling up now."

"Thank Geb!" Cleo held out her arms in a virtual hug, avoiding contact for fear of ruffling her feather bustier.

"Thank Geb is right," he said, returning the gesture.

"Gather!" announced Jaydra, the feared accessories editor. She jumped off the back of the intern's ATV and gathered her A-team. Her short bleached hair, yogurt-white skin, and gaudy cocktail ring on every finger gave Cleo some much-needed solace. The jewelry biz obviously wasn't as competitive as she had thought.

"The girls are here, and they're gorgeous! They just need a quick touch-up and wardrobe. Anything we don't get, we'll fix in post. Let's move! The sky is falling. Darkness is upon us."

Did she say "gorgeous"?

225

Cleo had always known that Blue and Clawdeen had a "look." Fetching? Yes. Intriguing? Absolutely. Exotic? One hundred percent. But gorgeous? By normie industry standards? Hmm, maybe the world was ready for change after all.

"Cleo!"

She turned happily. It was the first time she had been called something other than "the Egyptian" all day.

It was Melody Carver. In a leopard-print chiffon gown.

Has the world gone completely mad?

"What are *you* doing here?" she asked, looking past her shoulder, hoping to see the others pulling up the rear. But all she saw was a blond in a yellow dress and heels stumbling across the sand. "Where are the girls?"

"Did you really expect them to show up after what you did?" Melody asked. Her narrow gray eyes were squinty and accusatory.

"'Scuse me?" Cleo asked, her gold headdress clinking again. "I was told they were here."

"You were told wrong," Melody lifted a fallen spaghetti strap and draped it back over her shoulder.

"Will you please tell me what's happening? And start with why you are wearing a knockoff Roberto Cavalli dress."

The blond stepped forward. "First, it's not a knockoff. It's eighty-nine vintage. And second, you have some serious explaining to do."

"Who are *you*?" Cleo snipped, mindful not to tousle her blowout. "Stupid Boots Barbie?"

"This is Candace, my sister," Melody said. "And we're here representing NUDI to find out why you intentionally set out to destroy your friends. I would expect it from Bekka, but you? Do you have any idea what you've done? Everyone is—"

"Wow, Jaydra was right," gushed a pin-thin guy wearing red skinny jeans, a white tank top with an iron-on of King Tut, and three muslin scarves. "I'm Joffree. One name. And you girls *are* gorgeous. You must be from LA. Both size two, right?"

"I'm a zero on the bottom and a large on top." Candace winked.

"Let me pull some things. Be back faster than you can say Snuffleupagus."

"It's *sarcophagus*," Cleo corrected him for what felt like the billionth time.

"Omigod, men-tahl blahk," he sang as he scampered away.

"Melly, you didn't tell me we came here to *model*!" Candace beamed, smile-waving at the buff photographer.

"We didn't!" Melody snapped. "We came to get the truth."

"About *what*?" Cleo insisted. Everything around her was moving so quickly. Buzzing assistants. Missing friends. Gorgeous normies. False accusations. "I swear to Geb, I have no clue what you're talking about."

"'The Ghoul Next Door'? The unblurred interviews? Don't act like you don't know."

"I'm not *acting*!" shouted Cleo. She was in desperate need of more gloss.

"They aired! The unblurred interviews aired."

"Wait—*what*?" She stood completely still. "How is that possible?" Cleo asked frantically. "I was right there when—"

"Aha!" Melody clapped once. "So you *do* know something."

"I never wanted that stupid show to air even when the faces

were blurred. I knew it was dangerous. So why would I want it shown *unblurred*?" Cleo rubbed her throbbing temples. Her mind was playing catch-up. Still trying to figure out why her friends hadn't shown. Wondering how on earth such a catastrophe could have happened. Her friends would all be exposed!

The intern pulled up on her ATV, cupped her hands over her mouth, and yelled, "Joffree! Jaydra needs the new girls dressed and on the camels eight minutes ago."

"Then someone should have told me that nine minutes ago!" he huffed, sliding hangers along a wardrobe rack. "All right, New Girls, back here with me," he called.

"Coming!" Candace began her wobbly trek toward the racks.

"Stop!" Melody ordered. Her sister stopped instantly. "We didn't come here to model."

"Yes, you did," Cleo begged in a whisper. "Please, just do it. *Please.* I'll tell you everything I know. Swearsies on Ra." She lifted her face to the sinking sun. "We have to get through this— it won't take long. I'll even float you some samples from my new jewelry line the minute it gets off the ground."

"You promise?" Melody asked.

"Definitely. Are you more a tigereye kind of girl or straight-up gold?"

"No! Do you promise to tell me what you know about the TV show?"

"On all nine lives of all my cats."

While the Carver sisters were changing, Cleo tried to piece everything together. The show airing…unblurred…but how? She couldn't imagine Brett doing it behind Frankie's back. He seemed too genuine for something like that. Even if he had dated

Bekka, which Cleo still found hard to believe. What did someone like him ever see in...*omigoddess! Bekka!*

Melody emerged first. Wearing the typical black wig with bangs, she looked like Halloween Cleo, minus the sass. The gown, a sleeveless deep V made from layers of airy white silk and gold Lurex thread, luffed like a ship's sails in the early-evening breeze. Her gray eyes were heavily lined in turquoise kohl and adorned with gold false lashes. Even without the jewels, which would be fitted at the very last minute for security purposes, she defined Cairo-couture-meets-Babylon-babe.

"Hey," Cleo said with a half grin. "You look good...for you."

Melody smiled.

Finally.

"Marc Antony, Marc Antony, wherefore art thou, Marc Antony?" Candace called, scanning the tent with a hand on her forlorn heart. Her wig was the same as her sister's, but Candace's dress was gold, her kohl was black, and her fake lashes were dark jade. Jaydra was right: The Carver sisters were undeniably gorgeous. But Cleo was too grateful to be jealous. Besides, *her* hair was real! And that counted for something.

"Follow me." The intern hurried them through the tent and past the admiring eyes of the crew members. Even without the stares, Cleo knew the trio was *Vogue*-worthy.

"You'd better tell me what you know," Melody said out the side of her overglossed mouth. "'Cause I'd have no problem taking off this wig and going home."

"Fine." Cleo sighed and then came clean about her plan to erase the movie. Which, now that she was at the shoot, seemed insane. It was hard to believe she had almost done something that despicable just to be *there*, with a pack of overcaffeinated, underfed normies who had spent all day referring to her as "the Egyptian."

"So you're saying you didn't do anything?" Melody asked.

"I didn't have to. The show was canceled."

"So how—"

"Bekka," Cleo said. "She must have hacked into Brett's computer after I left."

"I told you not to trust her," Melody said.

"I didn't," Cleo said. "But I needed her."

Melody nodded slowly, identifying with Cleo, not judging her. "So, what do we do now?"

"I dunno. *Smile?*" she said sarcastically as they stepped onto the set.

"Whoa," said Candace. "I feel like I'm in one of those *beach-inside-a-bottle* things they sell at airport gift shops."

Cleo giggled. Candace was right. The sand had been dyed pink, yellow, and orange, and it was piled higher on the left than on the right, as if someone one was pouring it. Three camels sat at the lower end, legs tucked beneath them, chewing slowly and sighing.

"Unbelievable. That's *exactly* what I was going for," said a muscular man wearing a black tank top, camo cargoes, and a blond ponytail. "I'm Kolin VanVerbeentengarden." He extended a tanned hand to Candace. "But most people just call me Van-Verbeentengarden."

"Candace. But most people just call me awesome."

Cleo and Melody giggled.

"I'm going to add the bottle and the cork during postproduction," explained VanVerbeentengarden. "The concept is that you three are ancient Egyptian queens who washed ashore in this bottle and—"

"And we have come to present-day America on a mission to share these gems with today's modern teenager?" Candace finished.

"Precisely!" exclaimed VanVerbeentengarden.

"Yeah," Candace nodded. "I can totally see that."

"And I can totally see you and me getting together after this shoot." He winked.

"That depends," Candace teased.

"On what?"

"On how I look in the pictures."

She was good.

"The very least of my concerns." VanVerbeentengarden winked again as an assistant hooked a camera around his shoulder like an AK-47. Then the photographer turned his attention toward a case of lenses.

Overhead, a canopy of star-shaped lights flickered on, casting a magical twinkle across the shimmering sand. It was perfect. Aunt Nefertiti's jewels were going to love it.

"I never would have guessed that this was supposed to look like a bottle thingy," Cleo admitted.

"Me either," said Melody.

"Me either," said Candace. "I read it on Joffree's clipboard."

Cleo burst out laughing.

Melody just rolled her eyes in a *that's-Candace-for-you* sort of way.

"All right, girls, let's get you on these camels," the intern said.

The sisters exchanged nervous glances. But not Cleo. She had been on a camel at Zanzibar's petting zoo when she was seven.

And from what she remembered, it was no different from riding a slow, lumpy horse, which she'd also done at Zanzibar's.

"Stay on the path so you don't mess up the sand. Each animal has a sticker on his hump with your name and his name. Please claim your animal and wait for the wrangler. She'll help you up."

"That's what he said." Cleo giggled.

"Nice one." Candace slapped her five.

The closer they got to the camels, the more it smelled like wet hay and cat poo.

Candace winced. "Ew, what is that?"

"Camel butt," Melody said with a giggle.

"I think mine is sick," said Cleo. She pinched her nostrils and leaned closer to read the name on his hump. "Don't worry, Niles," she cooed, pulling a small atomizer from her cleavage. "This should help." She walked around the tan camel while spritzing amber fragrance into the stinky air. He sneezed. She spritzed. He sneezed. She spritzed.

"Can I try some of that?" Candace asked.

Cleo tossed her the perfume.

"Hey, Humphrey, it's not just you and the boys anymore." Candace sprayed. "You're in the presence of models. You have to smell your very best."

She tossed the bottle to Melody. After the first spritz, Luxor sneezed, rocked to his feet, and took off. Niles and Humphrey followed.

The girls jumped out of the way.

"Omigod, where's the wrangler?" shouted Jaydra as the camels sneezed and stampeded, kicking up the confection-colored sand. "Where is he?"

"*She* is right here!" shouted a stocky brunette in cowboy gear and black gloves. "What's happening?"

"My set!" shouted VanVerbeentengarden. "Do something, wrangler!"

"My name is *Kora*!" she said, readying the lasso that was clamped to her dungarees. "Jeez, you'd think someone with a name like VanVerbeentengarden could remember *Kora*."

"Just get them back. We're losing—"

"I know, we get it," she said, mounting an ATV. "You're losing light." She hit the gas and sped toward her flock. But the roar of the engine only scared the camels more.

Cleo and Candace locked arms and huddled together, sheltering each other from the whipping sand. But they refused to take cover in the tent, like the rest of the panicked crew. The chaos was far too entertaining.

"Start shooting, VanVerbeentengarden!" Jaydra shouted. "I'm not paying you to stare."

"What am I supposed to shoot?" VanVerbeentengarden shouted back. "I have no models, no jewels, and no visibility."

"Then shoot me!" Jaydra yelled, stuffing a finger-gun in her mouth.

"I've been wanting to all day," he huffed.

"Oats?" called Kora, tossing food as she roared by. "Who wants oats?" she called, gripping her lasso, preparing to launch. But camels weren't easily bribed with food—something a camel wrangler should have known.

"Niles, Humphrey, Luxor?" Someone called from the top of the rainbow-colored dune. "Niles, Humphrey, Luxor?" The voice had a musical quality to it—pure, clear, and angelic.

233

"Melly?" Candace gasped at the sight of her sister, lit to golden perfection by the sinking sun, white fabric rippling around her. She had the presence of a divine goddess.

"Niles, Humphrey, Luxor?" she sang.

Jaydra and VanVerbeentengarden stopped shouting.

The sound was like nothing Cleo had ever heard, yet something she imagined being standard in the afterlife.

"Nilesss, Humphreyyyy, Luxorrrrr?" Melody trilled.

The crew stopped scrambling. Even Candace was quiet.

"Nilesss, Humphreyyyy, Luxorrrrr?" Her irresistible singsong call was melodic silk, sailing over the darkening dunes. If Clawdeen had been there, she would have rolled onto her back in peaceful surrender.

Kora turned off the ATV.

"Nilesss, Humphreyyyy, Luxorrrrr, you're safe. Nilesss, Humphreyyyy, Luxorrrrr, you're safe. Come baaack."

The camels stopped running. They stopped sneezing, grunting, and bucking. "Nilesss, Humphreyyyy, Luxorrrrr, come back."

One by one, they did.

Kora raced over, hooked the camels with leashes, and led them back to their trailers.

"That's a wrap," Jaydra yelled, kicking a bag of oats. She stomped off in an *I-am-so-not-looking-at-your-jewelry-sketches* sort of way. Not that Cleo could blame her. The shoot had been a catastrophe. But far from disappointing.

Melody jumped off the dune and raced toward them, seemingly unfazed by her breathtaking performance.

"How did you do that?" Cleo asked, awestruck.

Crew members hurried by, wanting a closer look at the girl with the magical voice. But once they approached, they seemed nervous and unsure, as if they didn't know whether they should thank her or pray to her. So most of them just kept walking.

"I think your voice is back!" Candace hugged her sister tight. When they parted, their wigs were lopsided and mussed.

"Crazy, right?" Melody knit her dark brows. "I just called the camels. I had no idea what would come out. But it *was* kind of musical."

"I have to call Mom and Dad. They're going to freak," Candace said, hurrying away toward a table topped with camera gear.

"Why are you going over there to call them?" Melody asked.

"Because after I call, I'm going to ask VanVerbeentengarden if he takes yearbook pictures," Candace admitted with a guilty smirk.

Melody giggled.

"Can we go change? I'm having hoodie separation anxiety."

Cleo nodded. She would have done anything Melody had asked after what she'd just witnessed. Melodork was some sort of camel-whisperer! Cleo couldn't wait to forgive Deuce and then tell him all about it.

"Amazing," said Manu when the girls entered the tent. His eyes were misty. "That was absolutely amazing."

"Thanks," Melody said shyly.

"Is your mother here?" he asked.

"No, I came with my sister."

"Well." He sighed, like someone recalling a fond memory.

"Tell Marina that Manu says hi. It's been way too long." After a kind, lingering grin, he turned to Cleo. "I'm going to pack up the jewels. I'll meet you by the car."

"I think you have me confused with someone else," Melody said.

"Oh no," he scoffed. "That voice is unmistakable. Just like your mother's. Marina could get anyone to do absolutely anything; it was *that* intoxicating."

"Sorry, but my mom is Glory. Glory Carver. From California."

"Are you sure?"

"Manu, of course she's sure," Cleo snapped. "I think she knows who her mother is."

He was staring at Melody's face in a way that would have royally creeped Cleo out if she didn't know him. "Manu!"

He shook his head. "You're right. I *am* thinking of someone else."

Melody smiled forgivingly.

"I remember hearing that Marina's daughter had a very unforgettable nose. It almost looked like a camel's humps," he chuckled. "And yours is perfect. My mistake. I'm sorry."

He turned and left.

"I'm sorry too," Cleo said to Melody. "He's not usually that weird."

Melody didn't say a word.

"Oh, and I'm also sorry for not trusting you." She giggled. "Will you forgive me?"

Melody gazed blankly ahead.

"I'll stop calling you Melodork." Cleo batted her lashes playfully. "Hey!" she snapped. "Are you listening?"

But Melody didn't respond. She just stood there, staring at the passing camels and gripping her nose.

If Cleo hadn't been so anxious to make up with her friends and put this whole ordeal behind her, she might have asked her new recruit what was wrong. Instead, she hopped into her limo and hurried back to Salem. She had been gone only a few hours, but it felt like a lifetime since she'd been home.

CHAPTER TWENTY-SIX
MOM GENES

"NUDI duty done!" Candace peeled out of the dark parking lot and lifted her palm, expecting a triumphant sisterly slap.

"Hands on the wheel," Melody insisted.

Candace did what she was told. "Okay, so *that* was seriously amazing on every possible level *possible*!"

Ping!

TO: Melody
Oct 14, 8:19 PM
MOM: CANDACE TOLD ME YOUR VOICE IS COMING BACK!!!!
CAN'T WAIT TO HEAR. LOVE YOU!

Without responding, Melody tucked the phone inside the pocket of her hoodie.

"Can? Would you say my old nose looked like a camel's humps?" she asked, fixated on her reflection in the side-view mirror.

"Yeah," Candace said, giggling. "It kind of did. Hey, did you even know camels could run like that? I had no idea. Could you imagine if we had been on them? It's not like that wrangler could have saved us, that's for sure. She was so freaked, I think that poo smell was coming from her, not Humphrey. Too bad Van-Verbeentengarden didn't get any shots. He said he didn't want to get sand in his lenses, which I guess is for the best, 'cause he's taking my yearbook picture in the spring. Hey, maybe he can be the official NUDI photographer. He can ride with us on missions and document our battles. Too bad he didn't get you beating the truth out of Cleo. Love the girl and everything, I really do, but was she seriously going to erase that movie? Just to get her friends to that shoot? Omigod, even *I* wouldn't do that. And what about Joffree? Do you really think he was born without a last name?" She paused for a nanosecond. "Too bad VanVerbeentengarden wasn't...."

Melody tried to nod in all the right places. Tried to agree when Candace gave an opinion. Tried to smile at the charming parts. But everything came out sounding like a tiny grunt. She considered asking Candace if she'd ever heard of a Marina, a woman with a voice so intoxicating she "could get anyone to do absolutely anything." But maybe Manu had it all wrong. Maybe Marina was a distant aunt or her old nanny or the mother of some other kid with a camel-hump nose and a magical voice. Because Glory Carver was her mother, of that she was sure...until now.

"Okay, so here's my theory on Jaydra. For starters, her name is probably Jane Drake, or something boring like that. And Jane Drake had terrible style until one day she landed a job in a clothing store, probably thanks to some relative. But it wasn't a cool store like Intermix or the Co-Op. It was cool by *her* standards, like bebe or Betsey Johnson. After a few months, she started getting discounts and bought some clothes. She'd copy the other, cooler salesgirls until one day, during her lunch break, someone at the food court complimented her outfit. And that rocked her world. That night she changed her name from Jane Drake to Jaydra and..."

Melody sighed, wishing she had never met Manu. She had earned Cleo's respect. There would no longer be a divide. RADs and the NUDIs could finally band together as a unified force. And they would need to, now more than ever. She had everything she had been fighting for.

Everything except the truth.

Don't miss what happens next!

MONSTER HIGH 3

Where There's a Wolf, There's a Way

Coming in fall 2011!